WATTERS • LEYH • ROGERS • LAIHO

LUMBERJANES™

MIND OVER METTLE

Published by

BOOM! BOX™

Ross Richie..CEO & Founder
Joy Huffman...CFO
Matt Gagnon..Editor-in-Chief
Filip Sablik..................President, Publishing & Marketing
Stephen Christy.............................President, Development
Lance Kreiter..............Vice President, Licensing & Merchandising
Arune Singh...........................Vice President, Marketing
Bryce Carlson.............Vice President, Editorial & Creative Strategy
Kate Henning....................................Director, Operations
Spencer Simpson..Director, Sales
Scott Newman...........................Manager, Production Design
Elyse Strandberg.................................Manager, Finance
Sierra Hahn..Executive Editor
Jeanine Schaefer....................................Executive Editor
Dafna Pleban...Senior Editor
Shannon Watters......................................Senior Editor
Eric Harburn...Senior Editor
Sophie Philips-Roberts..............................Associate Editor
Amanda LaFranco...................................Associate Editor
Jonathan Manning..................................Associate Editor
Gavin Gronenthal....................................Assistant Editor
Gwen Waller..Assistant Editor

Allyson Gronowitz...................................Assistant Editor
Ramiro Portnoy......................................Assistant Editor
Kenzie Rzonca.......................................Assistant Editor
Shelby Netschke.......................................Editorial Assistant
Michelle Ankley.....................................Design Coordinator
Marie Krupina.......................................Production Designer
Grace Park...Production Designer
Chelsea Roberts......................................Production Designer
Samantha Knapp.............................Production Design Assistant
José Meza..Live Events Lead
Stephanie Hocutt...............................Digital Marketing Lead
Esther Kim...Marketing Coordinator
Breanna Sarpy....................................Live Events Coordinator
Amanda Lawson.......................................Marketing Assistant
Holly Aitchison..................................Digital Sales Coordinator
Morgan Perry......................................Retail Sales Coordinator
Megan Christopher.................................Operations Coordinator
Rodrigo Hernandez.................................Operations Coordinator
Zipporah Smith.....................................Operations Assistant
Jason Lee...Senior Accountant
Sabrina Lesin.......................................Accounting Assistant

BOOM! BOX™

LUMBERJANES Volume Sixteen, December 2020. Published by BOOM! Box, a division of Boom Entertainment, Inc. Lumberjanes is ™ & © 2020 Shannon Watters, Grace Ellis, Noelle Stevenson & Brooklyn Allen. Originally published in single magazine form as LUMBERJANES No. 61-64. ™ & © 2019 Shannon Watters, Grace Ellis, Noelle Stevenson & Brooklyn Allen. All rights reserved. BOOM! Box™ and the BOOM! Box logo are trademarks of Boom Entertainment, Inc., registered in various countries and categories. All characters, events, and institutions depicted herein are fictional. Any similarity between any of the names, characters, persons, events, and/or institutions in this publication to actual names, characters, and persons, whether living or dead, events, and/or institutions is unintended and purely coincidental. BOOM! Box does not read or accept unsolicited submissions of ideas, stories, or artwork.

BOOM! Studios, 5670 Wilshire Boulevard, Suite 400, Los Angeles, CA 90036-5679. Printed in USA. First Printing.

ISBN: 978-1-68415-616-0, eISBN: 978-1-64668-028-3

THIS LUMBERJANES FIELD MANUAL BELONGS TO:

NAME:

TROOP:

DATE INVESTED:

FIELD MANUAL TABLE OF CONTENTS

LUMBERJANES
FIELD MANUAL

For the Intermediate Program

Tenth Edition • April 1985

Prepared for the

Miss Qiunzella Thiskwin
Penniquiqul Thistle Crumpet's

CAMP FOR  HARDCORE LADY-TYPES

"Friendship to the Max!"

A MESSAGE FROM THE LUMBERJANES HIGH COUNCIL

miss Quinzella Thiskwin
Penniquiqul Thistle Crumpet's
Camp for
HARDCORE LADY TYPES
FRIENDSHIP to the MAX!

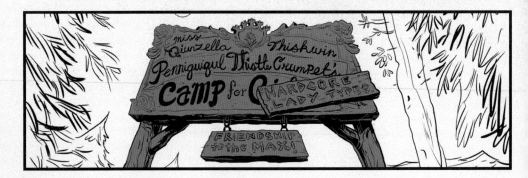

When you are working toward a goal, the image of your success is bright and vivid in your mind. You fall asleep at night imagining where you'll be in just a few months or years, or you fantasize about the future while you wait for the bus, or brush your teeth. It starts to feel almost like reality, like it is just barely out of your reach. Just a half step away from your current life.

But the truth is that nothing is guaranteed. A half a step forward can become a half a step to the left or right, or even a half step back, and suddenly everything that was on the precipice of coming together falls apart. The puzzle pieces that you were assembling are all scrambled, their picture irreconcilable with the one you had in your head.

We of the high council do not say this to upset you young and eager Lumberjanes, who we know all hold your own hopes and dreams dear to your hearts. Rather, we wish to share with you the knowledge that even when it seems like everything is going wrong, and even when it feels like the only options before you are bad and worse, there are ways through and help to be had. You may not always see it from the outset, but just like you could never have predicted how things would break apart, you also cannot know how they will come back together again.

After all, dissonance is only one note away from harmony. But even if you continue to move away from that first, glorious note, the one you thought was perfect, and that you cherished in your mind, you will eventually find another harmonic tone. Perhaps not the original one, or the one that you had hoped for, but one that is just as beautiful, in its own way.

THE LUMBERJANES PLEDGE

I solemnly swear to do my best
Every day, and in all that I do,
To be brave and strong,
To be truthful and compassionate,
To be interesting and interested,
To pay attention and question
The world around me,
To think of others first,
To always help and protect my friends,
[redacted]
And to make the world a better place
For Lumberjane scouts
And for everyone else.

THEN THERE'S A LINE ABOUT GOD, OR WHATEVER

MIND OVER METTLE

Written by
Shannon Watters
& Kat Leyh

Illustrated by
AnneMarie Rogers

Colors by
Maarta Laiho

Letters by
Aubrey Aiese

Cover by
Kat Leyh

Designer
Marie Krupina

Editor
Sophie Philips-Roberts

Executive Editor
Jeanine Schaefer

*Special thanks to **Kelsey Pate** for giving the Lumberjanes their name.*

Created by
Shannon Watters, Grace Ellis, Noelle Stevenson & Brooklyn Allen

LUMBERJANES FIELD MANUAL

CHAPTER SIXTY-ONE

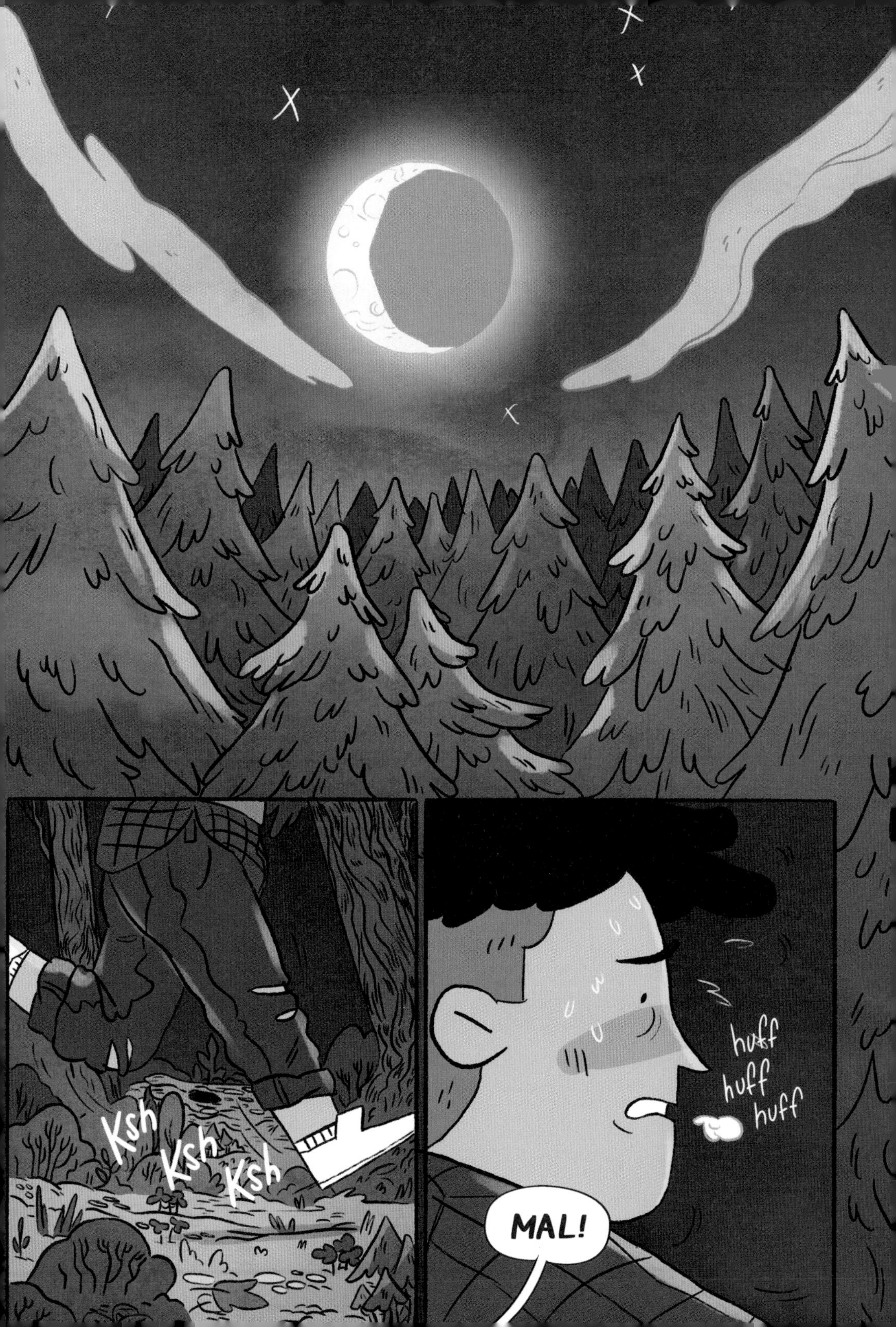
Ksh
Ksh
Ksh
huff
huff
huff
MAL!

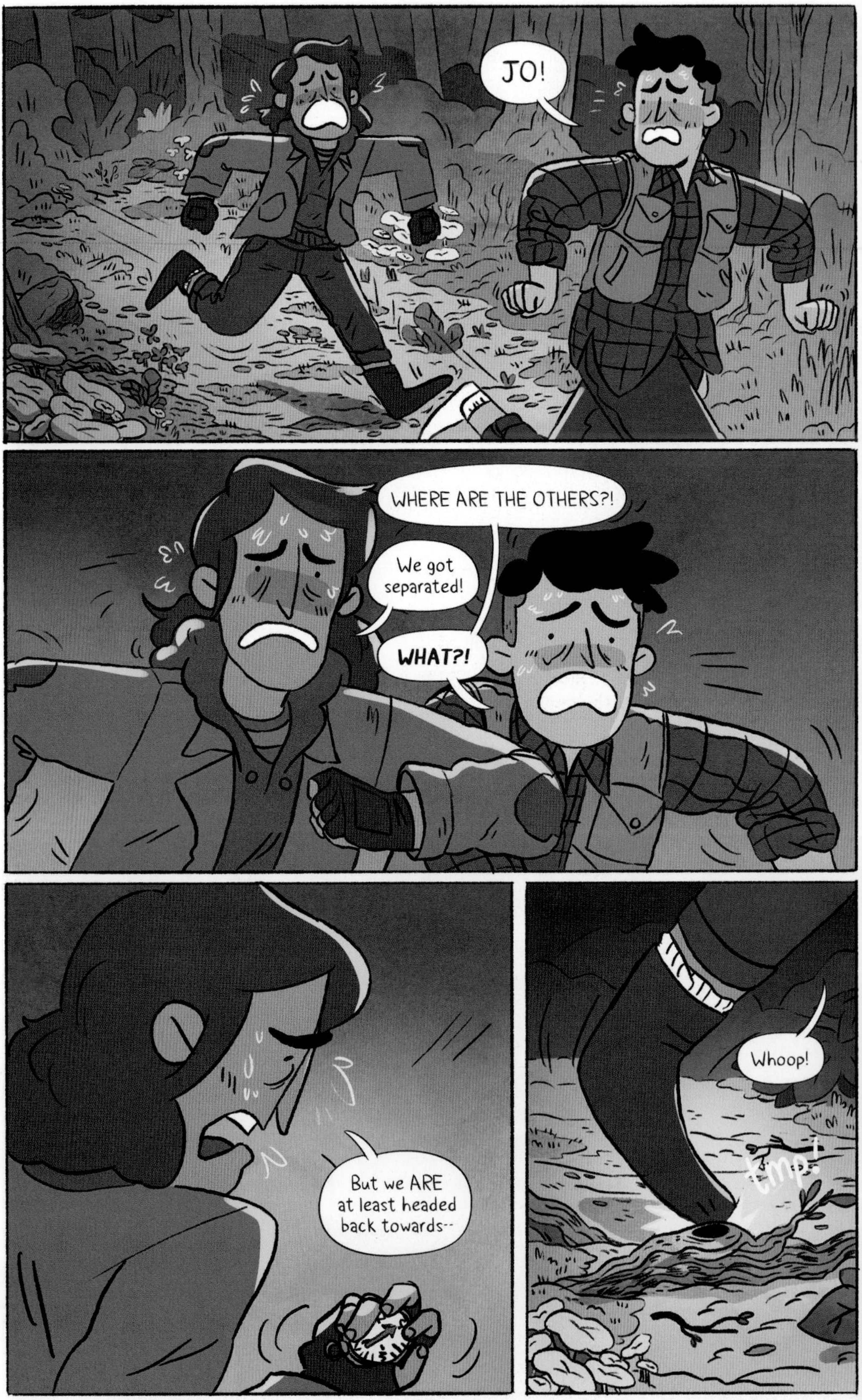
JO!
WHERE ARE THE OTHERS?!
We got separated!
WHAT?!
But we ARE at least headed back towards--
Whoop!
tmp!

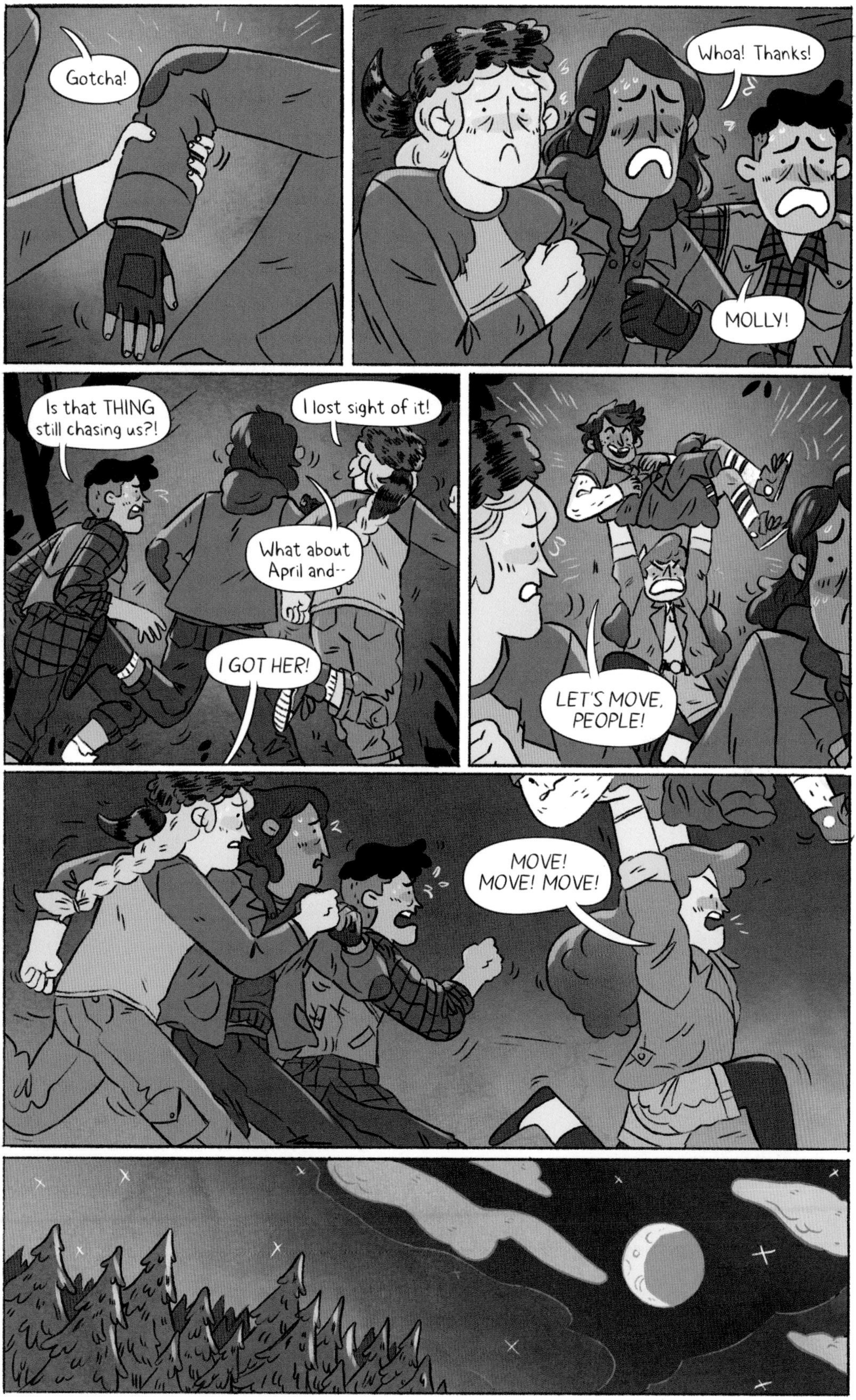
Gotcha!
Whoa! Thanks!
MOLLY!
Is that THING still chasing us?!
I lost sight of it!
What about April and--
I GOT HER!
LET'S MOVE, PEOPLE!
MOVE! MOVE! MOVE!

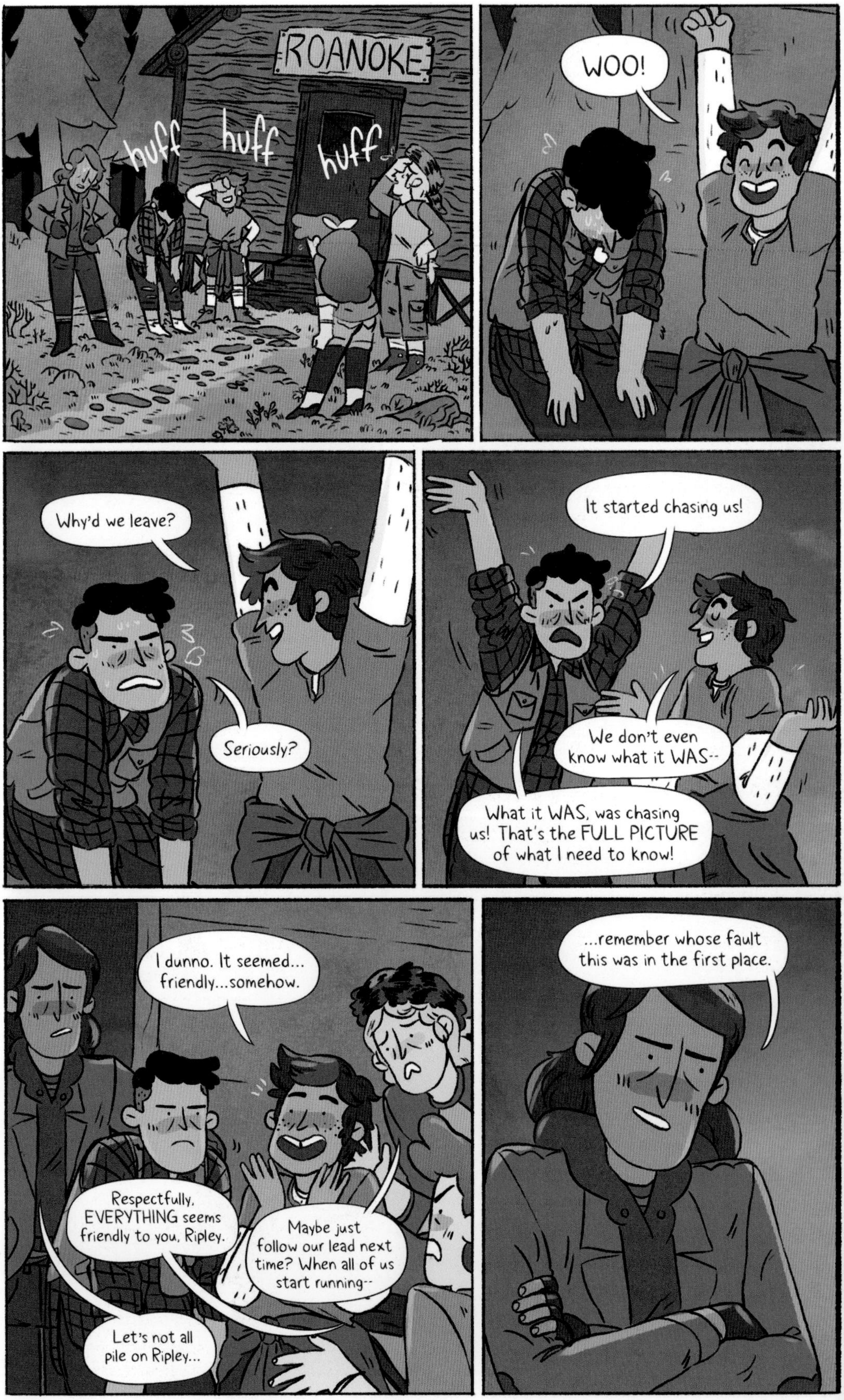
ROANOKE
huff
huff
huff
WOO!
Why'd we leave?
Seriously?
It started chasing us!
We don't even know what it WAS--
What it WAS, was chasing us! That's the FULL PICTURE of what I need to know!
I dunno. It seemed... friendly...somehow.
Respectfully, EVERYTHING seems friendly to you, Ripley.
Maybe just follow our lead next time? When all of us start running--
Let's not all pile on Ripley...
...remember whose fault this was in the first place.

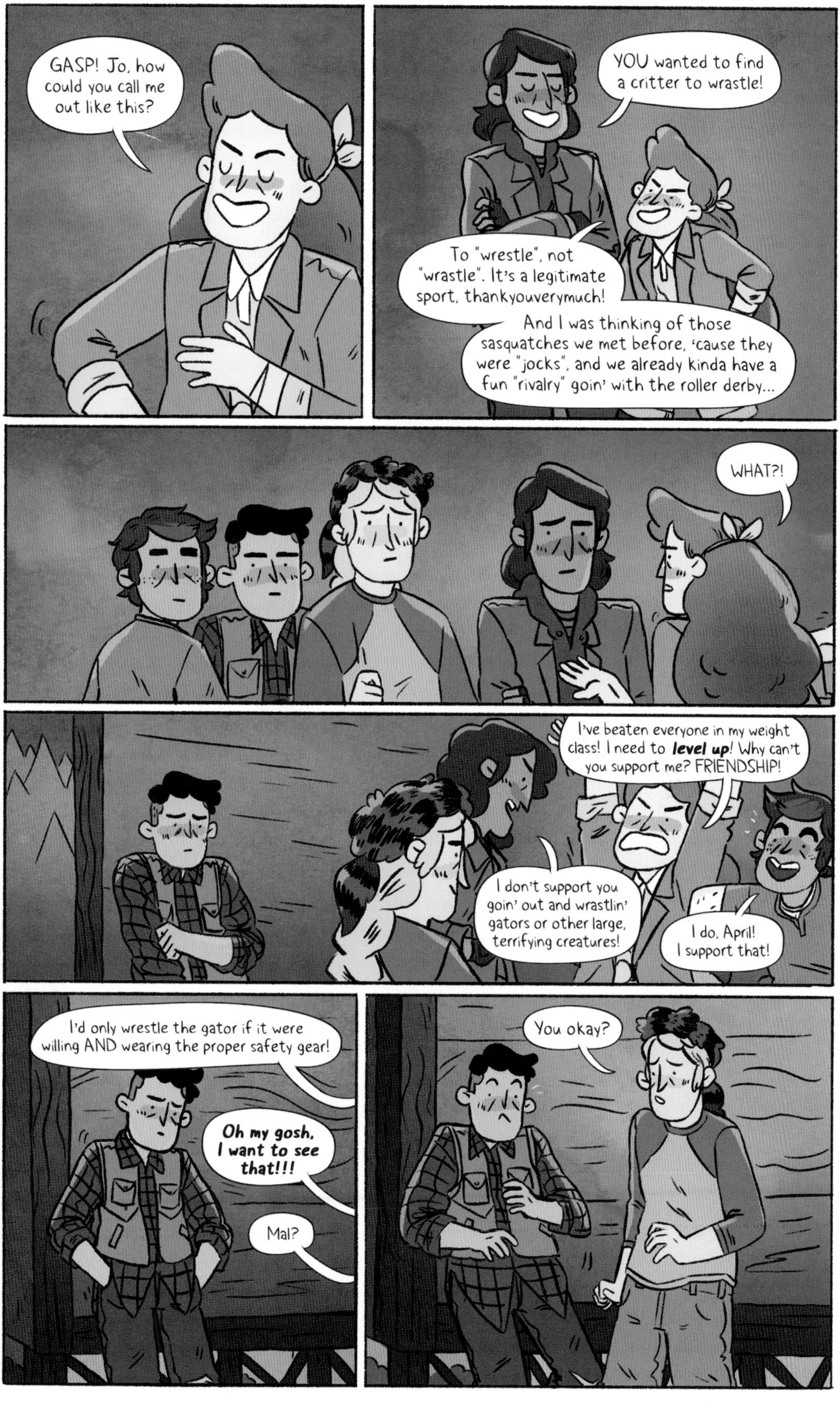
GASP! Jo, how could you call me out like this?
YOU wanted to find a critter to wrastle!
To "wrestle", not "wrastle". It's a legitimate sport, thankyouverymuch!
And I was thinking of those sasquatches we met before, 'cause they were "jocks", and we already kinda have a fun "rivalry" goin' with the roller derby...
WHAT?!
I've beaten everyone in my weight class! I need to **level up**! Why can't you support me? FRIENDSHIP!
I don't support you goin' out and wrastlin' gators or other large, terrifying creatures!
I do, April! I support that!
I'd only wrestle the gator if it were willing AND wearing the proper safety gear!
Oh my gosh, I want to see that!!!
Mal?
You okay?

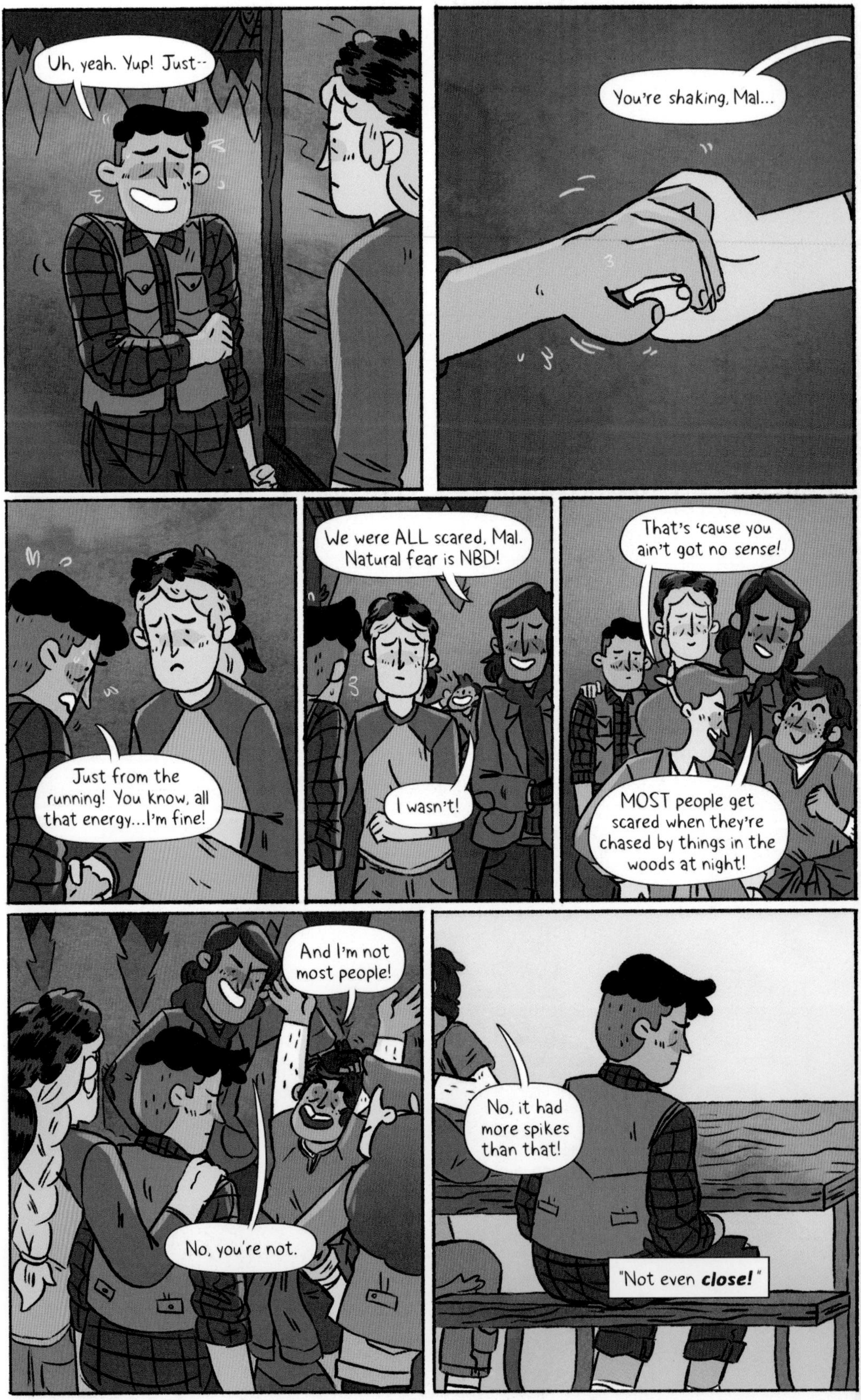
Uh, yeah. Yup! Just--
You're shaking, Mal...
Just from the running! You know, all that energy...I'm fine!
We were ALL scared, Mal. Natural fear is NBD!
I wasn't!
That's 'cause you ain't got no sense!
MOST people get scared when they're chased by things in the woods at night!
And I'm not most people!
No, you're not.
No, it had more spikes than that!
"Not even **close!**"

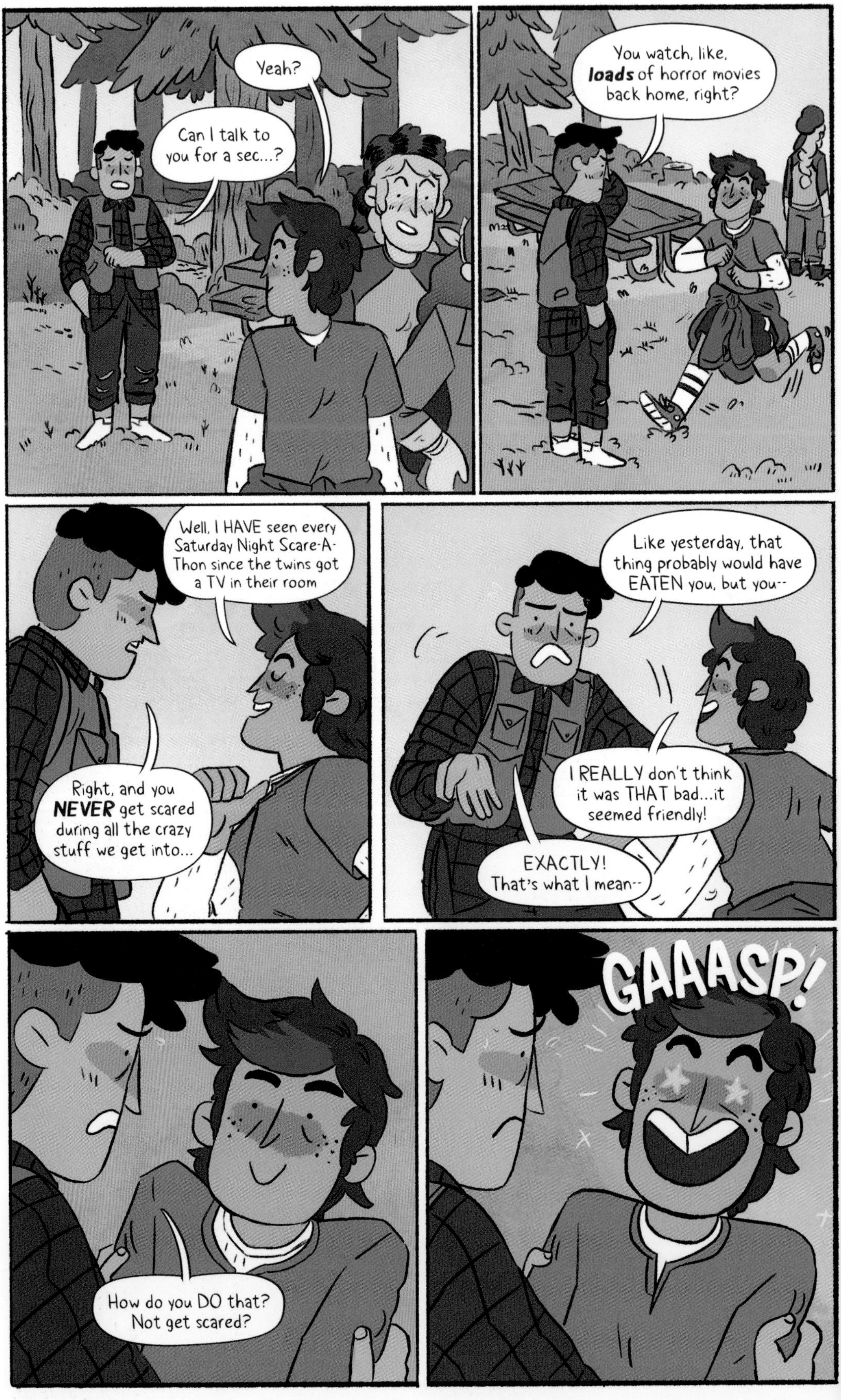
Can I talk to you for a sec...?
Yeah?
You watch, like, **loads** of horror movies back home, right?
Well, I HAVE seen every Saturday Night Scare-A-Thon since the twins got a TV in their room
Right, and you **NEVER** get scared during all the crazy stuff we get into...
Like yesterday, that thing probably would have EATEN you, but you--
I REALLY don't think it was THAT bad...it seemed friendly!
EXACTLY! That's what I mean--
How do you DO that? Not get scared?
GAAASP!

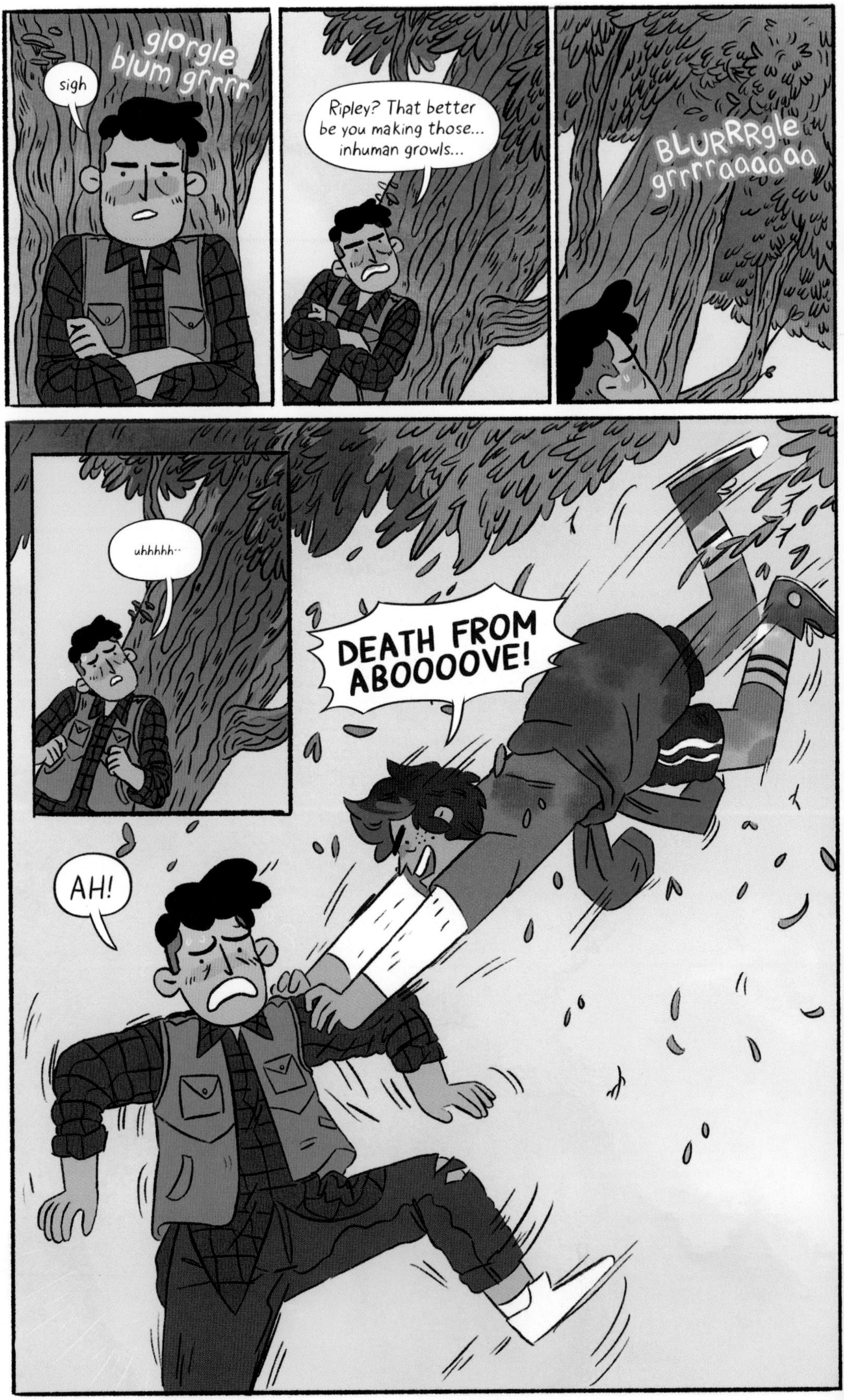
glorgle blum grrrr
sigh
Ripley? That better be you making those... inhuman growls...
BLURRRgle grrrraaaaaa
uhhhhh--
DEATH FROM ABOOOOVE!
AH!

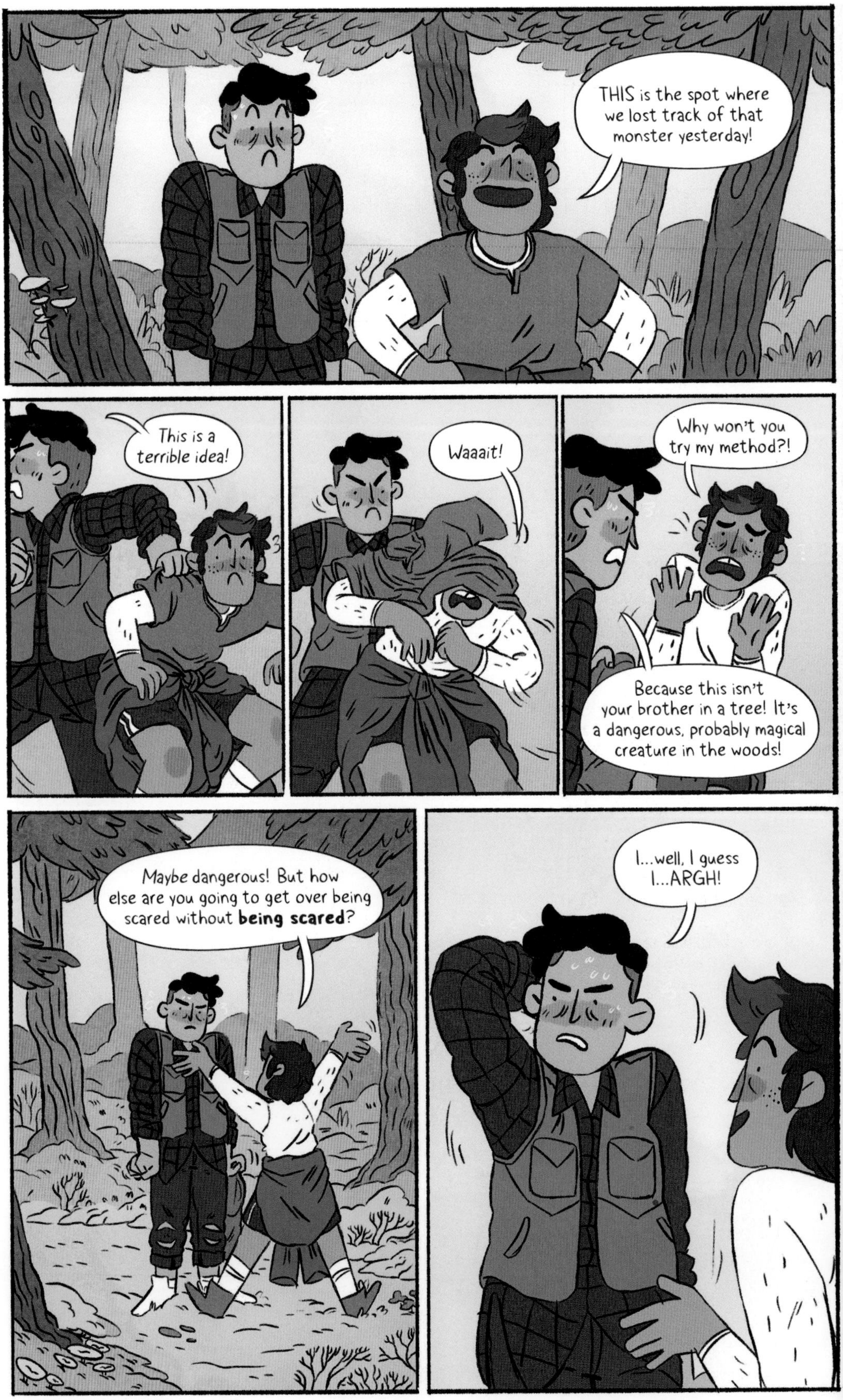
THIS is the spot where we lost track of that monster yesterday!
This is a terrible idea!
Waaait!
Why won't you try my method?!
Because this isn't your brother in a tree! It's a dangerous, probably magical creature in the woods!
Maybe dangerous! But how else are you going to get over being scared without **being scared**?
I...well, I guess I...ARGH!

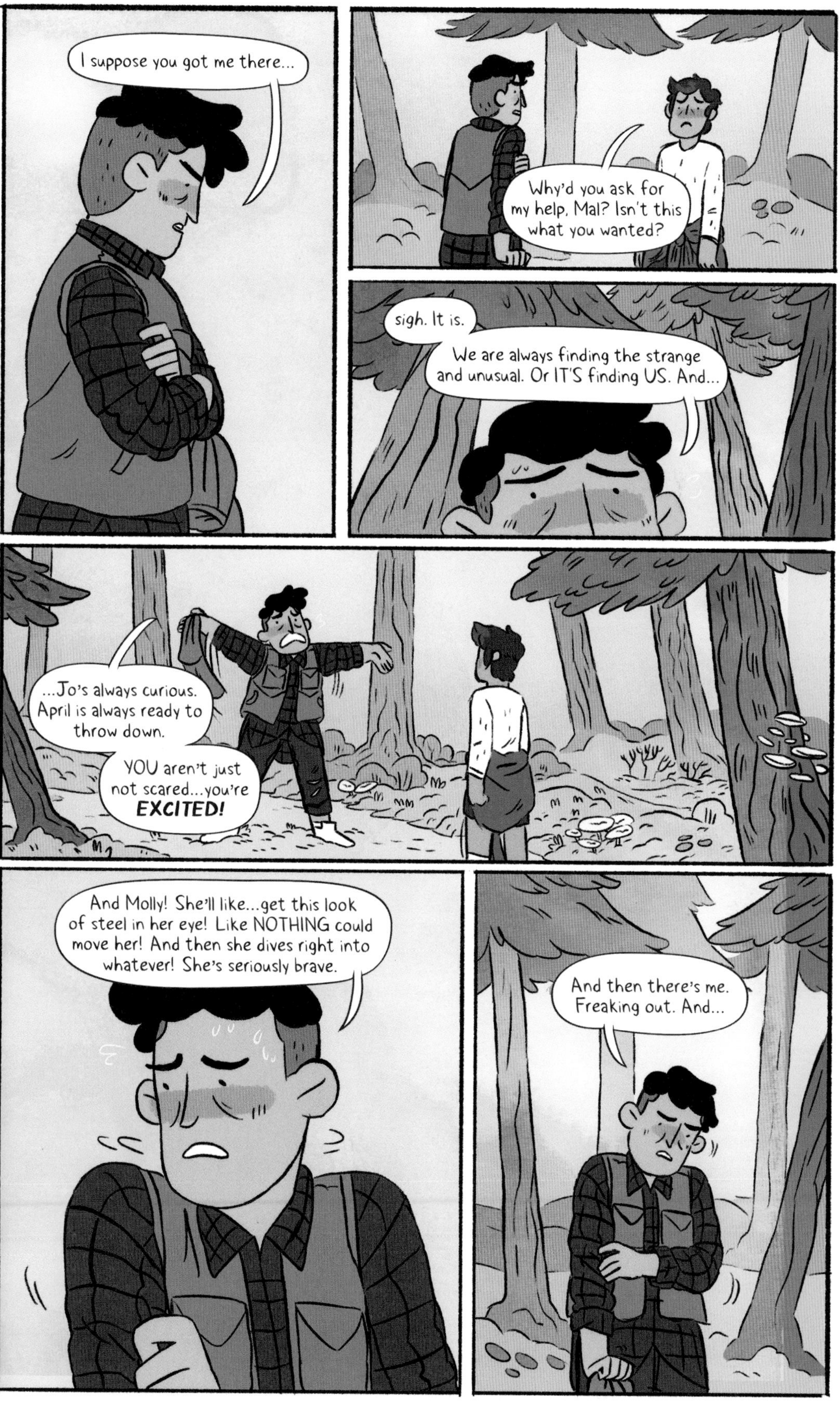

I suppose you got me there...
Why'd you ask for my help, Mal? Isn't this what you wanted?
sigh. It is.
We are always finding the strange and unusual. Or IT'S finding US. And...
...Jo's always curious. April is always ready to throw down.
YOU aren't just not scared...you're **EXCITED!**
And Molly! She'll like...get this look of steel in her eye! Like NOTHING could move her! And then she dives right into whatever! She's seriously brave.
And then there's me. Freaking out. And...

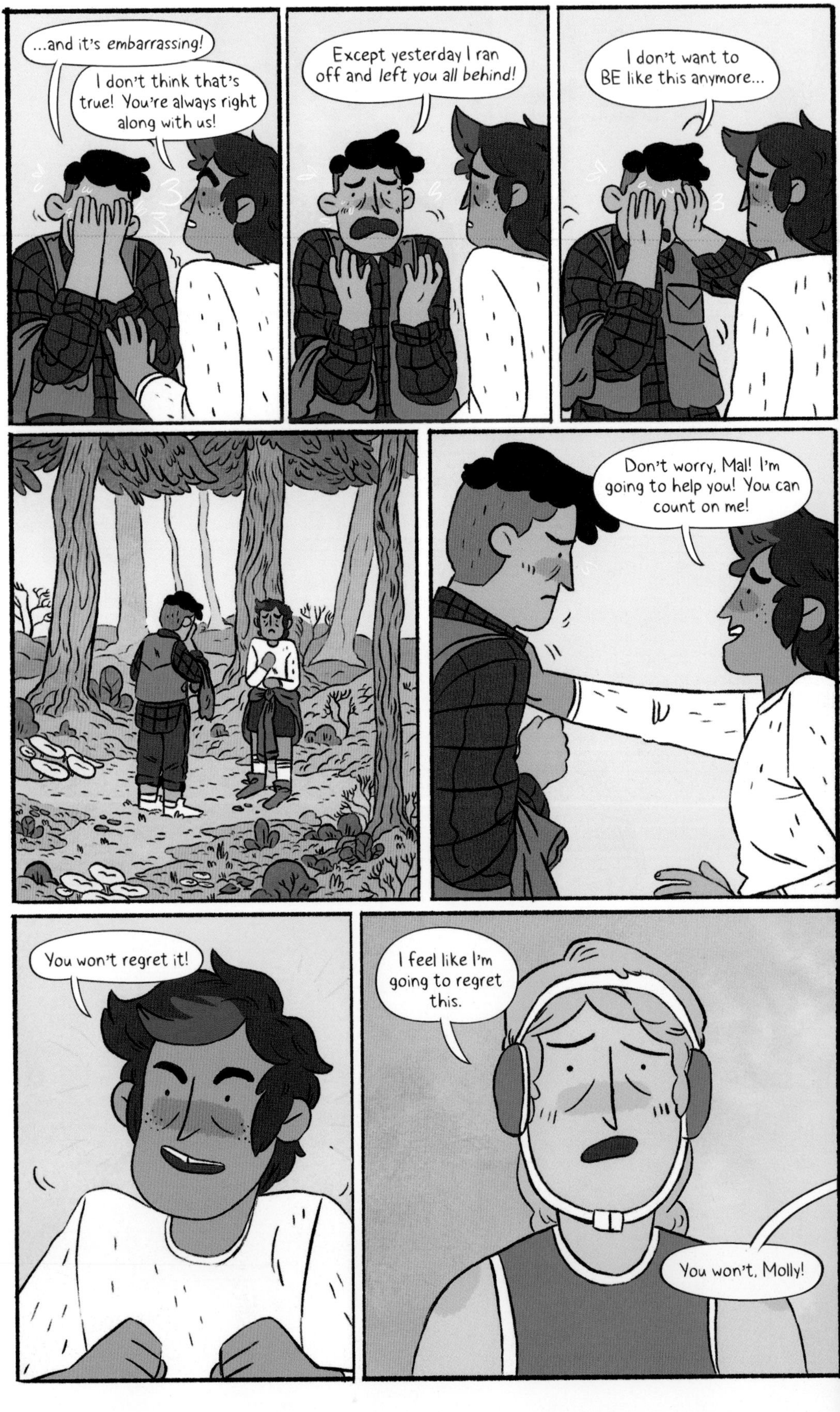
...and it's *embarrassing!*
I don't think that's true! You're always right along with us!
Except yesterday I ran off and *left you all behind!*
I don't want to BE like this anymore...
Don't worry, Mal! I'm going to help you! You can count on me!
You won't regret it!
I feel like I'm going to regret this.
You won't, Molly!

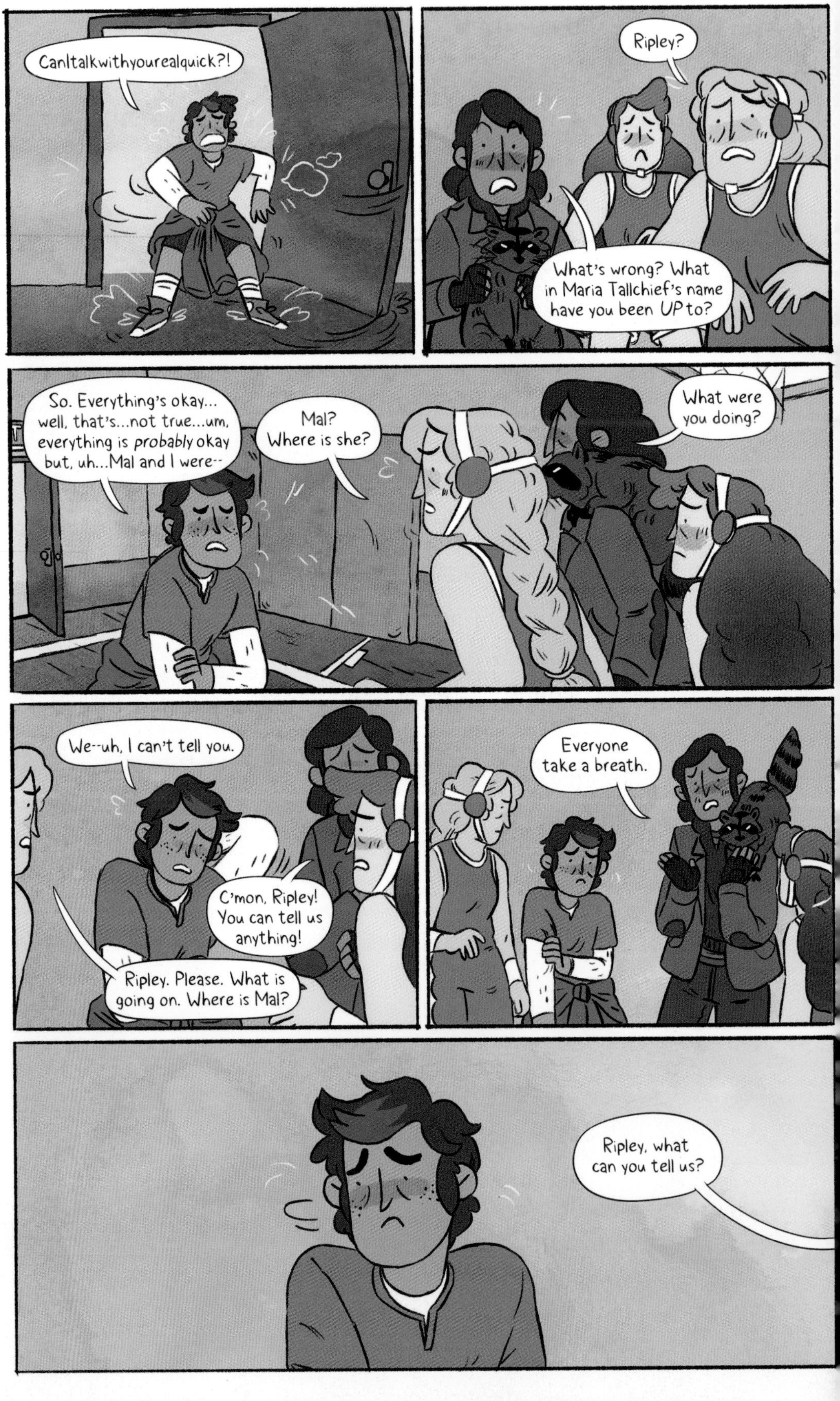

CanItalkwithyourealquick?!
Ripley?
What's wrong? What in Maria Tallchief's name have you been UP to?
So. Everything's okay... well, that's...not true...um, everything is probably okay but, uh...Mal and I were--
Mal? Where is she?
What were you doing?
We--uh, I can't tell you.
C'mon, Ripley! You can tell us anything!
Ripley. Please. What is going on. Where is Mal?
Everyone take a breath.
Ripley, what can you tell us?

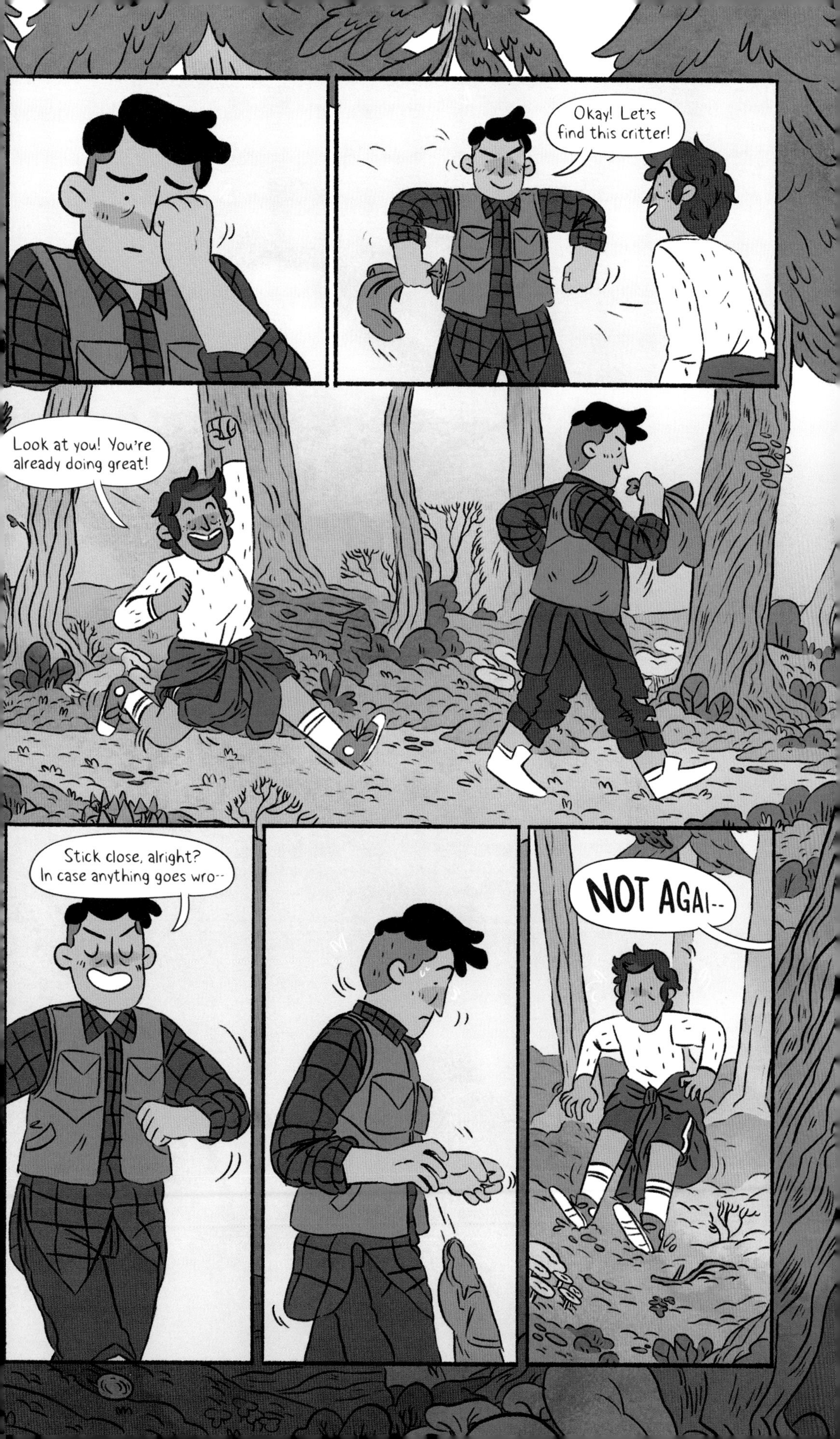

Okay! Let's find this critter!
Look at you! You're already doing great!
Stick close, alright? In case anything goes wro--
NOT AGAI--

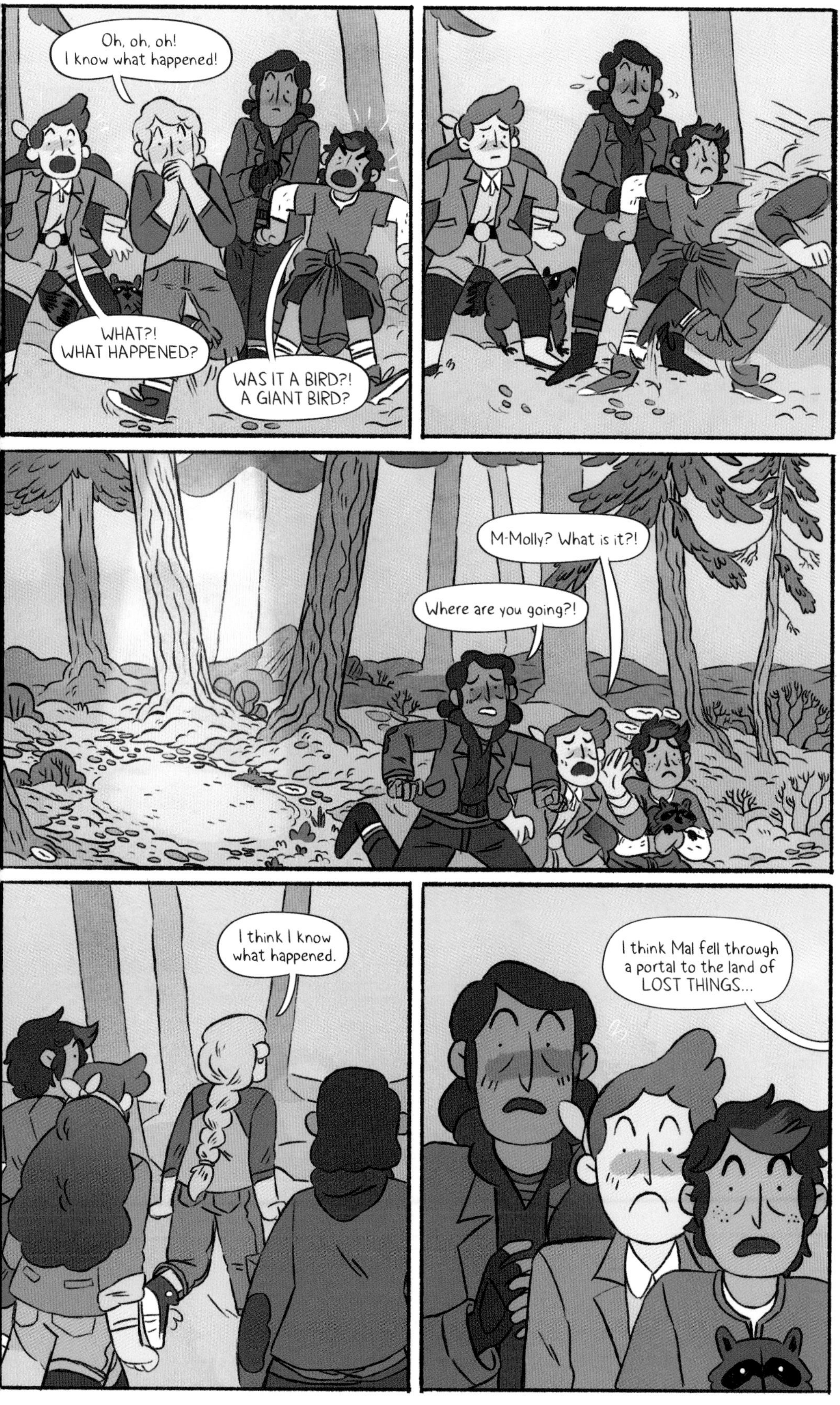
Oh, oh, oh!
I know what happened!
WHAT?!
WHAT HAPPENED?
WAS IT A BIRD?!
A GIANT BIRD?
M-Molly? What is it?!
Where are you going?!
I think I know
what happened.
I think Mal fell through
a portal to the land of
LOST THINGS...

will co...

The...
It he...
appearan...
dress f...
Further...
Lumber...
to have...
part in...
Thisw...
Hardc...
have...
them...

The...
yellow, short sl...
emb...
the w...
choose...
slacks,...
made o...
out-of-do...
green bere...
the colla...
Shoes ma...
heels, roun...
socks shoul...
the uniform. Ne...es, bracelets, or other jewelry do...
belong with a Lumberjane uniform.

HOW TO WEAR THE UNIFORM

To look well in a uniform demands first of...
uniform be kept in good condition—clean...
pressed. See that the skirt is the right length for your own
height and build, that the belt is adjusted to your waist,
that your shoes and stockings are in keeping with the
uniform, that you watch your posture and carry yourself
with dignity and grace. If the beret is removed indoors,
be sure that your hair is neat and kept in place with an
inconspicuous clip or ribbon. When you wear a
Lumberjane uniform you are identified as a member of
this organization and you should be doubly careful to
conduct yourself in a way that will show everyone that
courtesy and thoughtfulness are part of being a
Lumberjane. People are likely to judge a whole nation by
the selfishness of a few individuals, to criticize a whole
family because of the misconduct of one member, and to
feel unkindly toward an organization because of the

...HE UNIFORM
...should be worn at camp
...events when Lumberjanes
...may also be worn at other
...ions. It should be worn as a
...the uniform dress with
...rect shoes, and stocking or
...out grows her uniform or
...ng f...ther Lumberjane.
...a she has
...her
...her

The unifor...
helps to cre...
in a group. ...
active life th...
another bond...
future, and pr...
in order to b...
Lumberjane pr...
Penniquiqul Thi... ...ore Lady
Types, but m... ...es will wish to have one. They
can either b... ...niform, or make it themselves from
materials available at the trading post.

LUMBERJANES FIELD MANUAL

CHAPTER
SIXTY-TWO

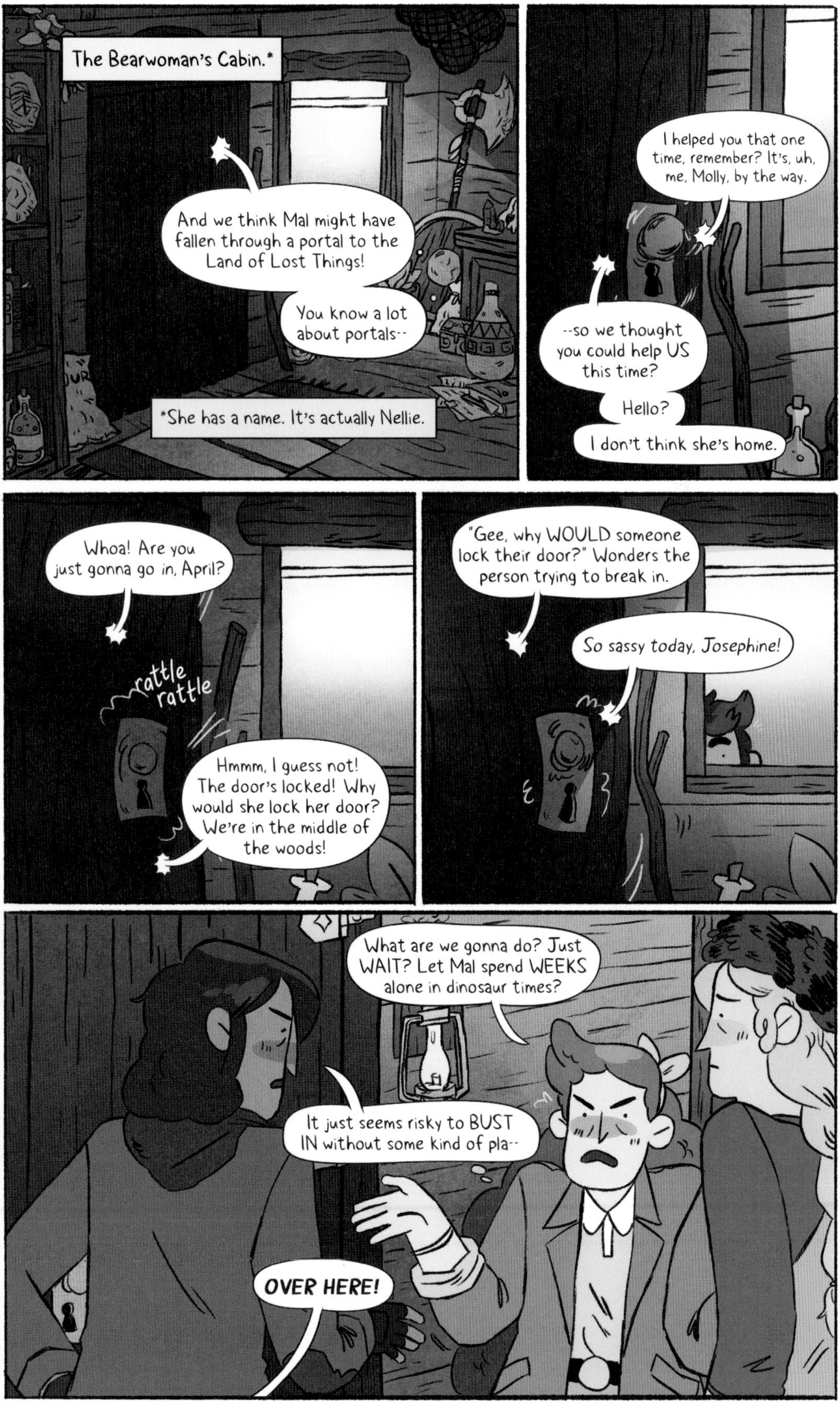
The Bearwoman's Cabin.*
And we think Mal might have fallen through a portal to the Land of Lost Things!
You know a lot about portals--
*She has a name. It's actually Nellie.
I helped you that one time, remember? It's, uh, me, Molly, by the way.
--so we thought you could help US this time?
Hello?
I don't think she's home.
Whoa! Are you just gonna go in, April?
rattle rattle
Hmmm, I guess not! The door's locked! Why would she lock her door? We're in the middle of the woods!
"Gee, why WOULD someone lock their door?" Wonders the person trying to break in.
So sassy today, Josephine!
What are we gonna do? Just WAIT? Let Mal spend WEEKS alone in dinosaur times?
It just seems risky to BUST IN without some kind of pla--
OVER HERE!

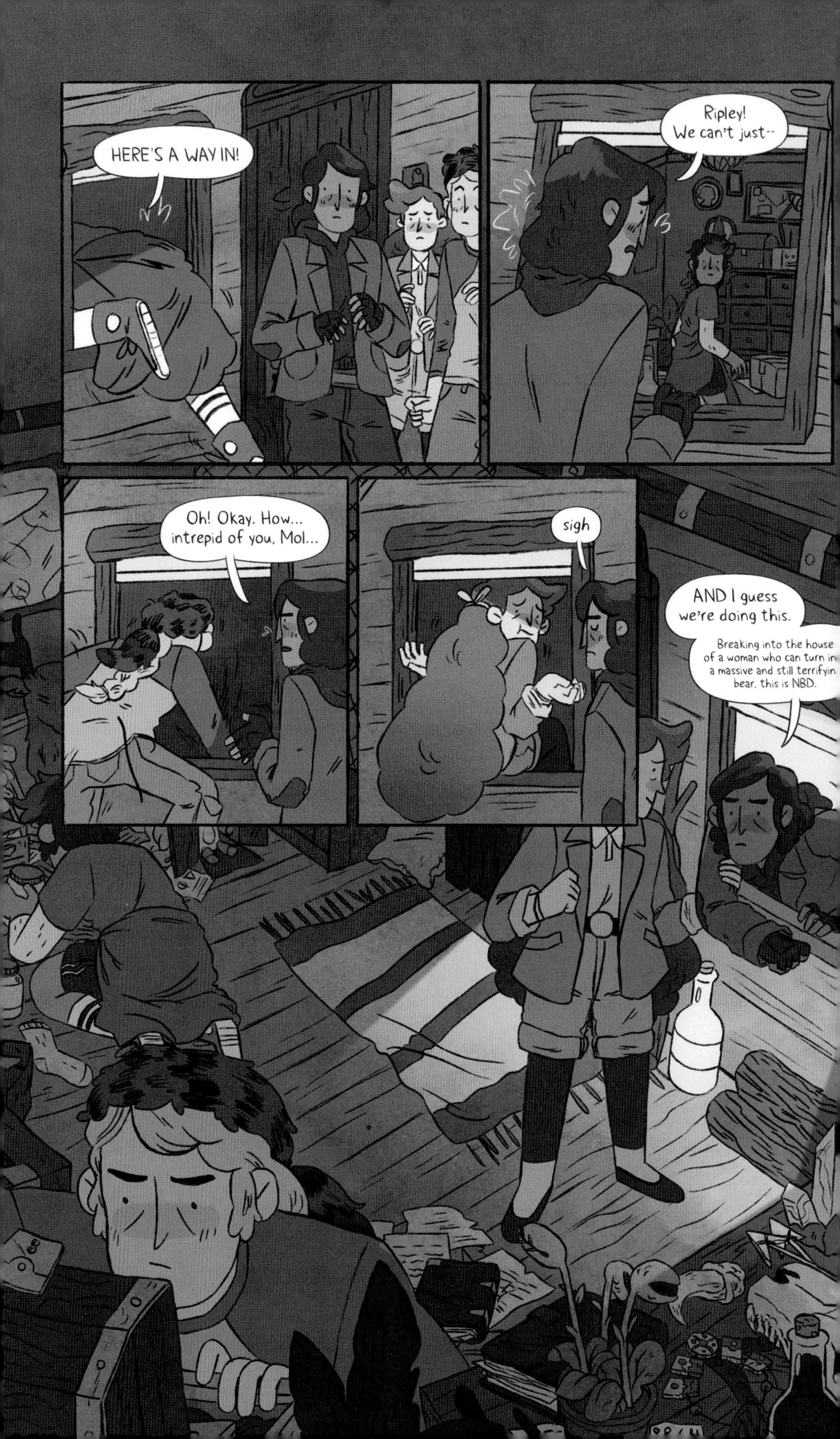
HERE'S A WAY IN!
Ripley! We can't just--
Oh! Okay. How... intrepid of you, Mol...
sigh
AND I guess we're doing this.
Breaking into the house of a woman who can turn in a massive and still terrifyin bear, this is NBD.

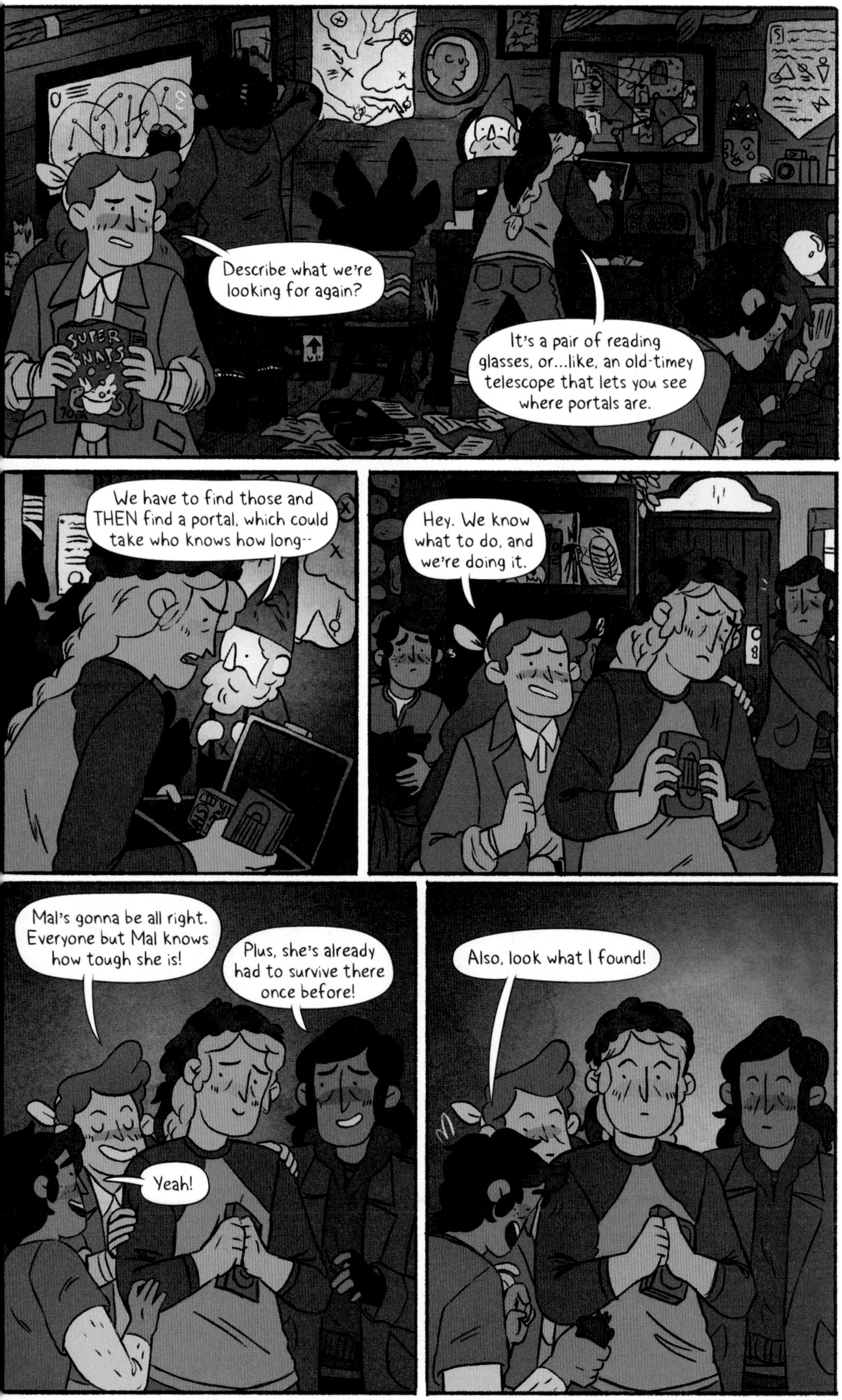
SUPER SNAPS
Describe what we're looking for again?
It's a pair of reading glasses, or...like, an old-timey telescope that lets you see where portals are.
We have to find those and THEN find a portal, which could take who knows how long--
Hey. We know what to do, and we're doing it.
Mal's gonna be all right. Everyone but Mal knows how tough she is!
Plus, she's already had to survive there once before!
Yeah!
Also, look what I found!

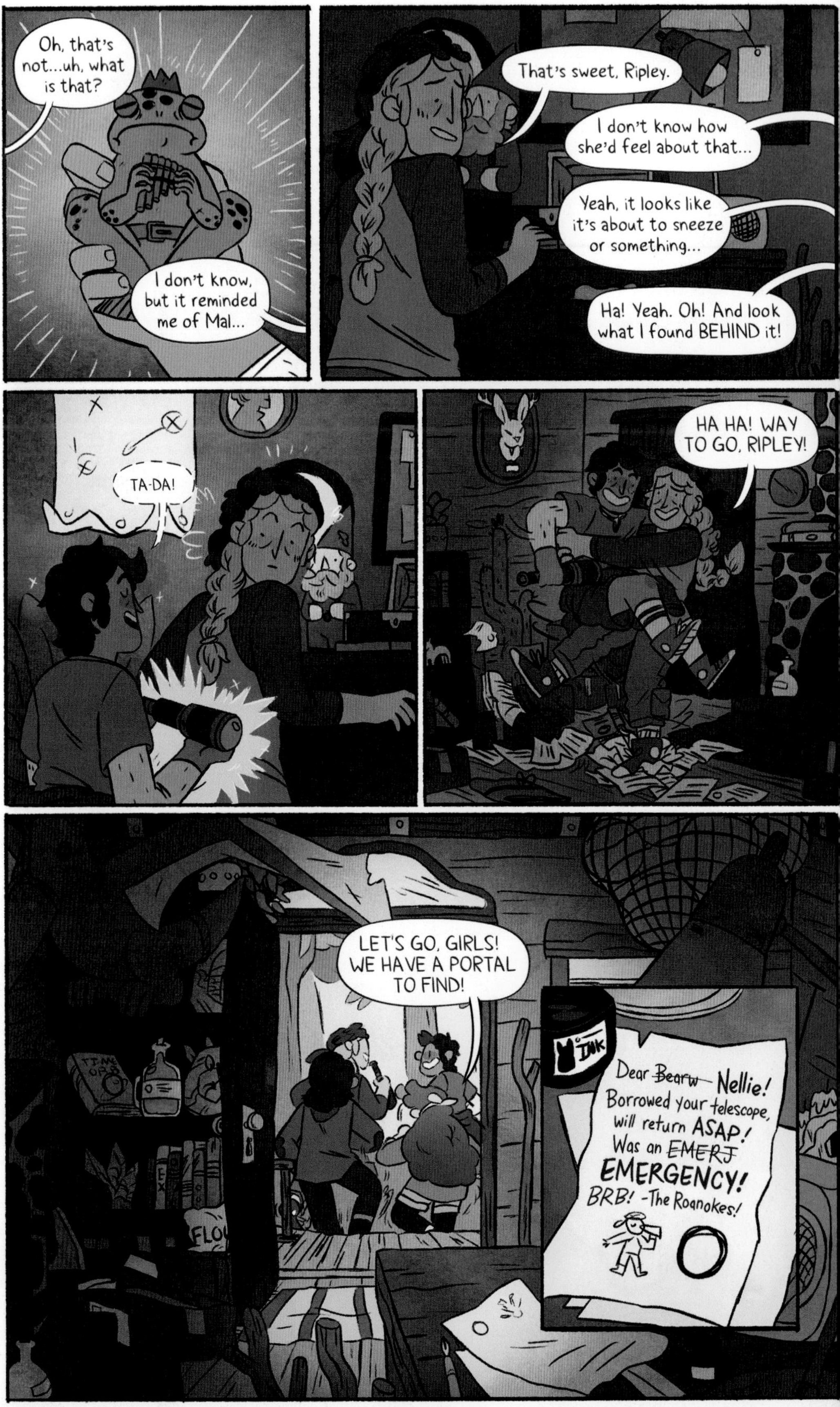

Oh, that's not...uh, what is that?
I don't know, but it reminded me of Mal...
That's sweet, Ripley.
I don't know how she'd feel about that...
Yeah, it looks like it's about to sneeze or something...
Ha! Yeah. Oh! And look what I found BEHIND it!
TA-DA!
HA HA! WAY TO GO, RIPLEY!
LET'S GO, GIRLS! WE HAVE A PORTAL TO FIND!
INK
Dear ~~Bearw~~ Nellie!
Borrowed your telescope, will return ASAP!
Was an ~~EMERJ~~ EMERGENCY!
BRB! -The Roanokes!

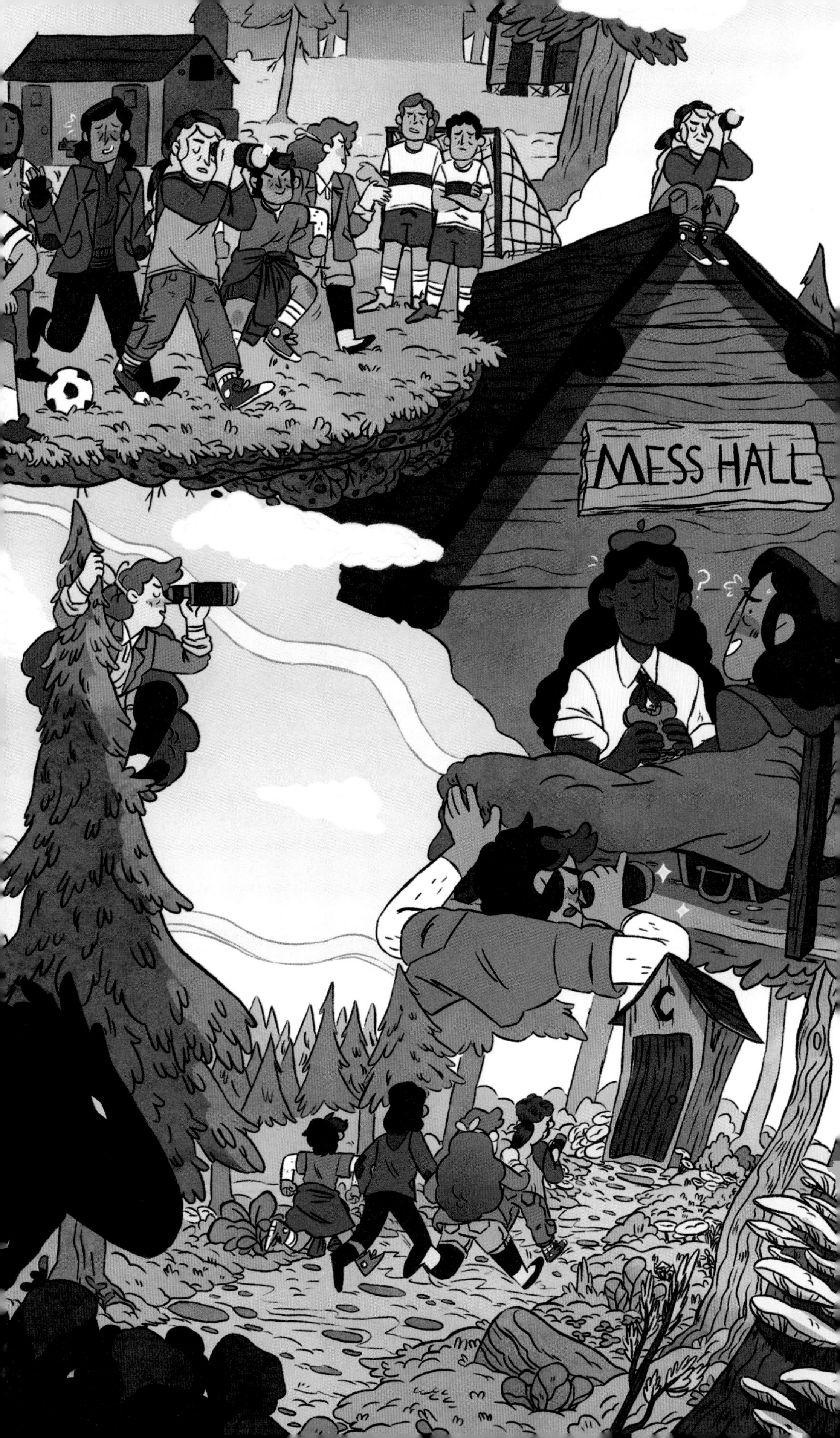
MESS HALL
C

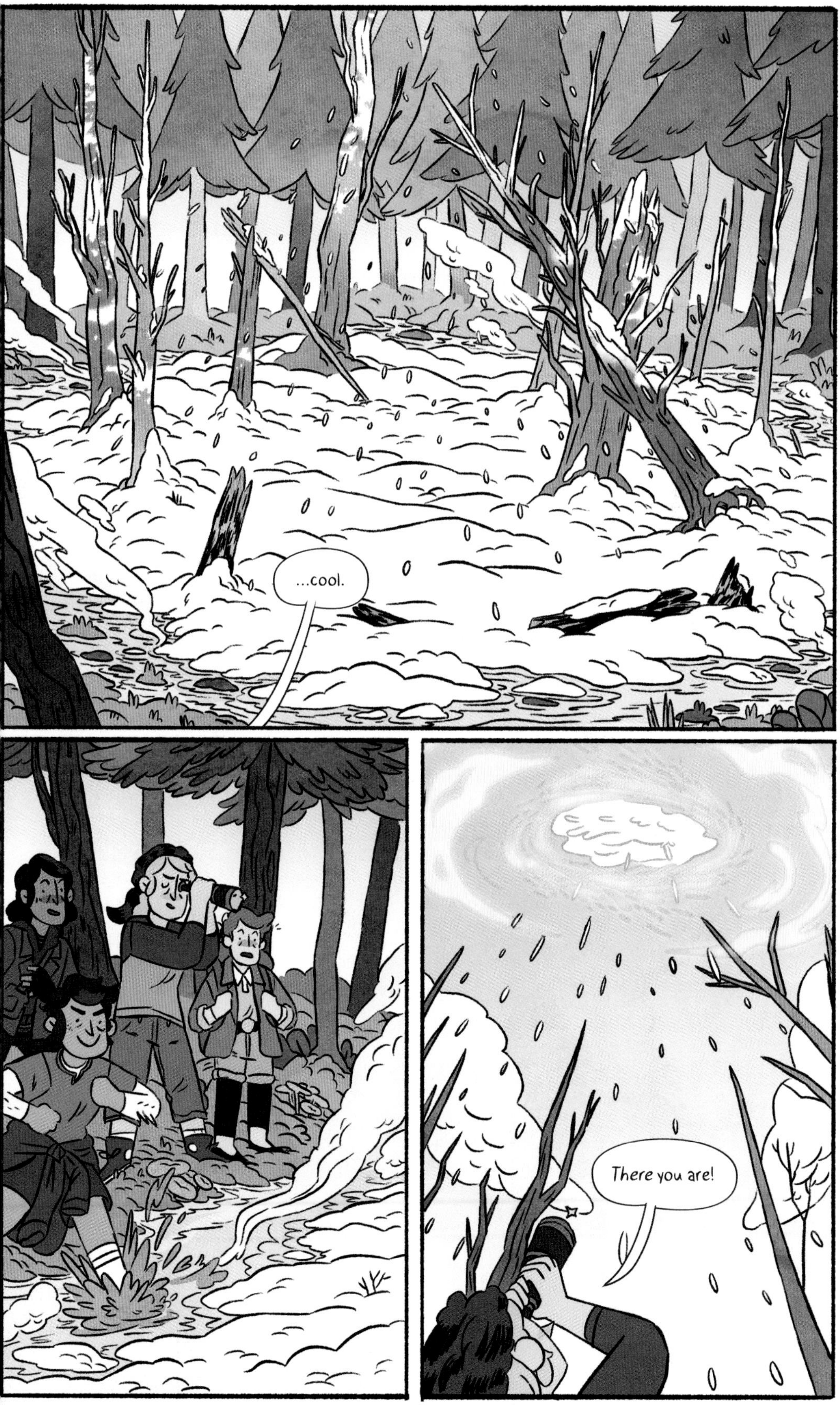
...cool.
There you are!

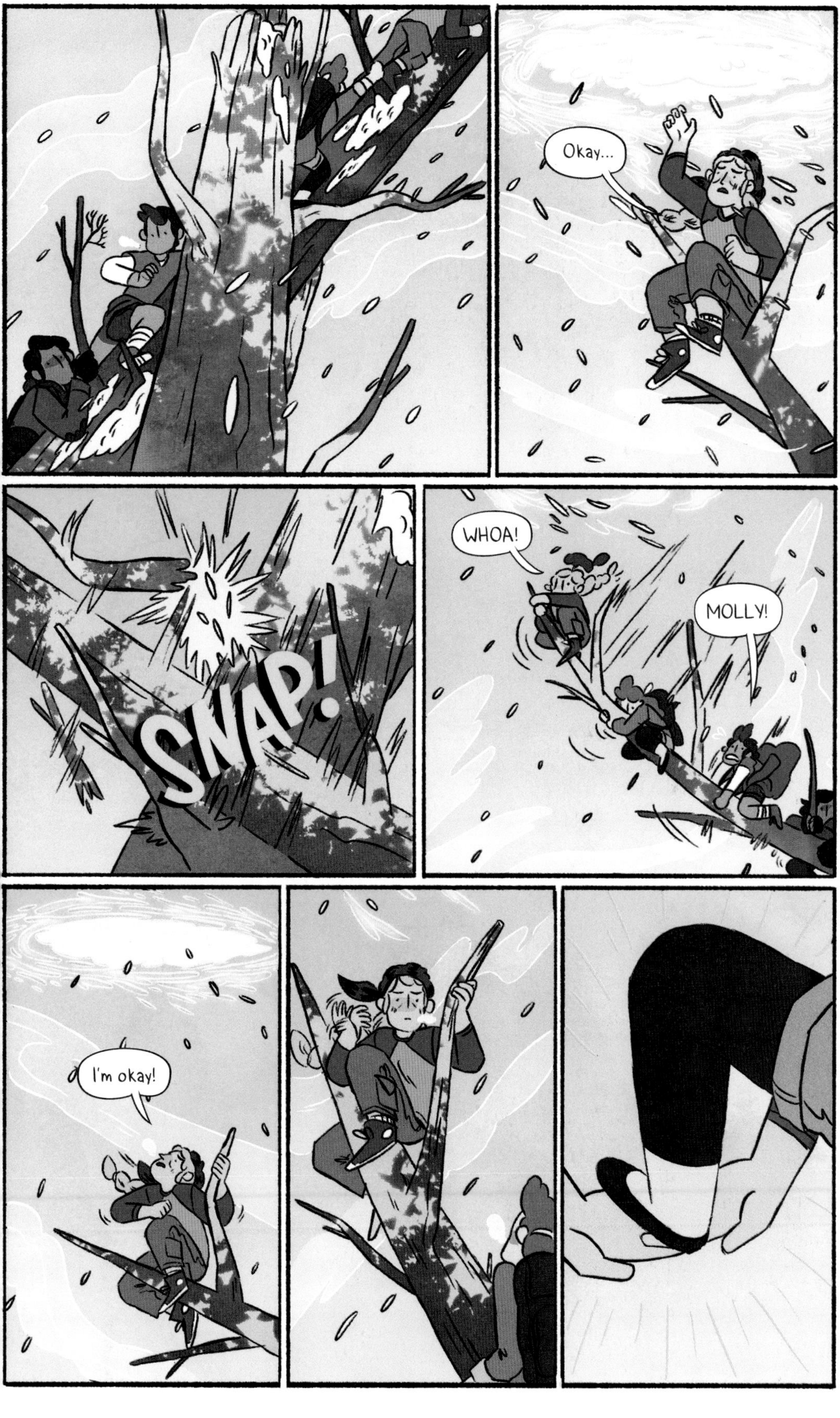
Okay...
SNAP!
WHOA!
MOLLY!
I'm okay!

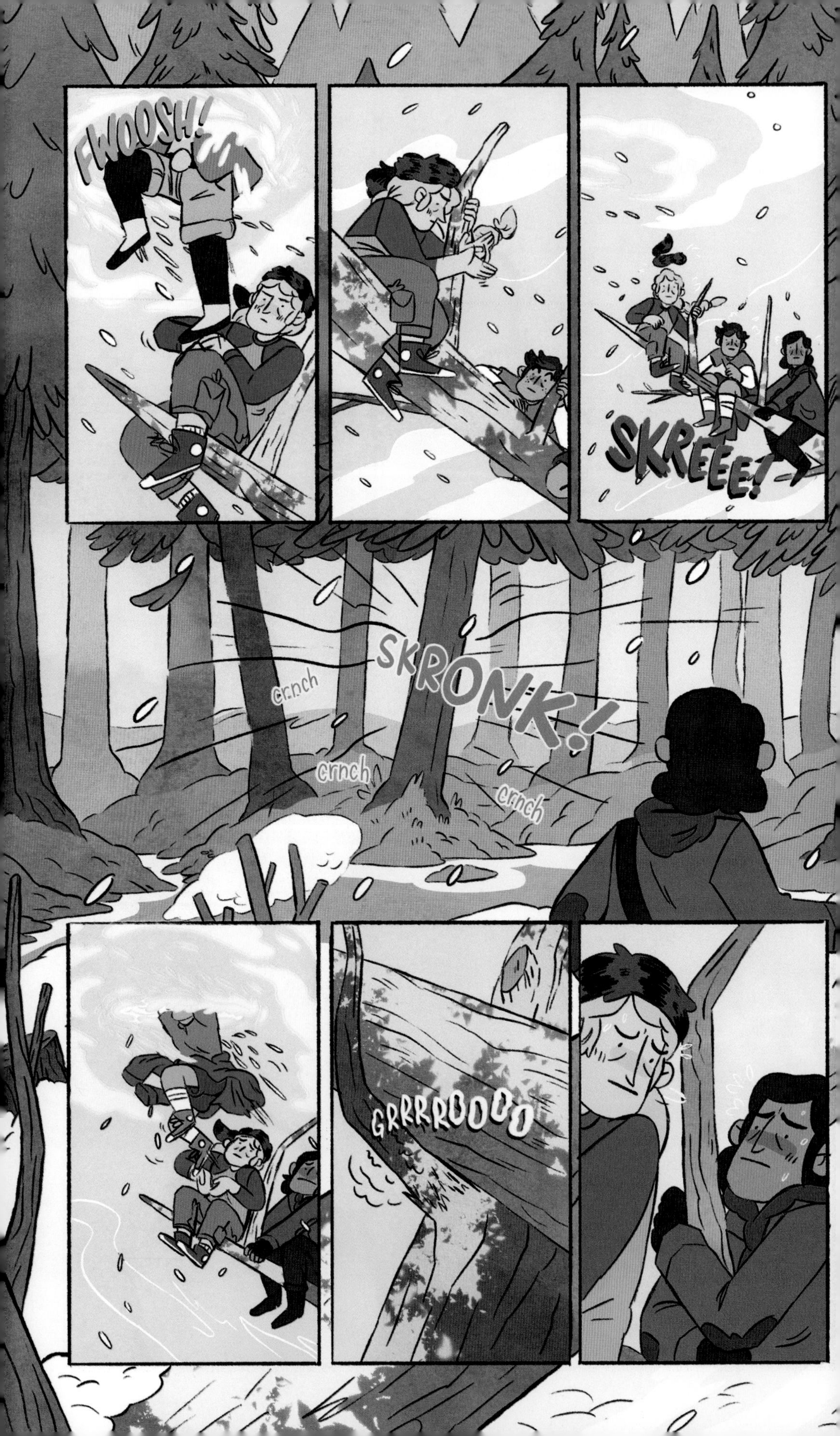
FWOOSH!
SKREEEE!
SKRONK!
crnch
crnch
crnch
GRRRROOOO

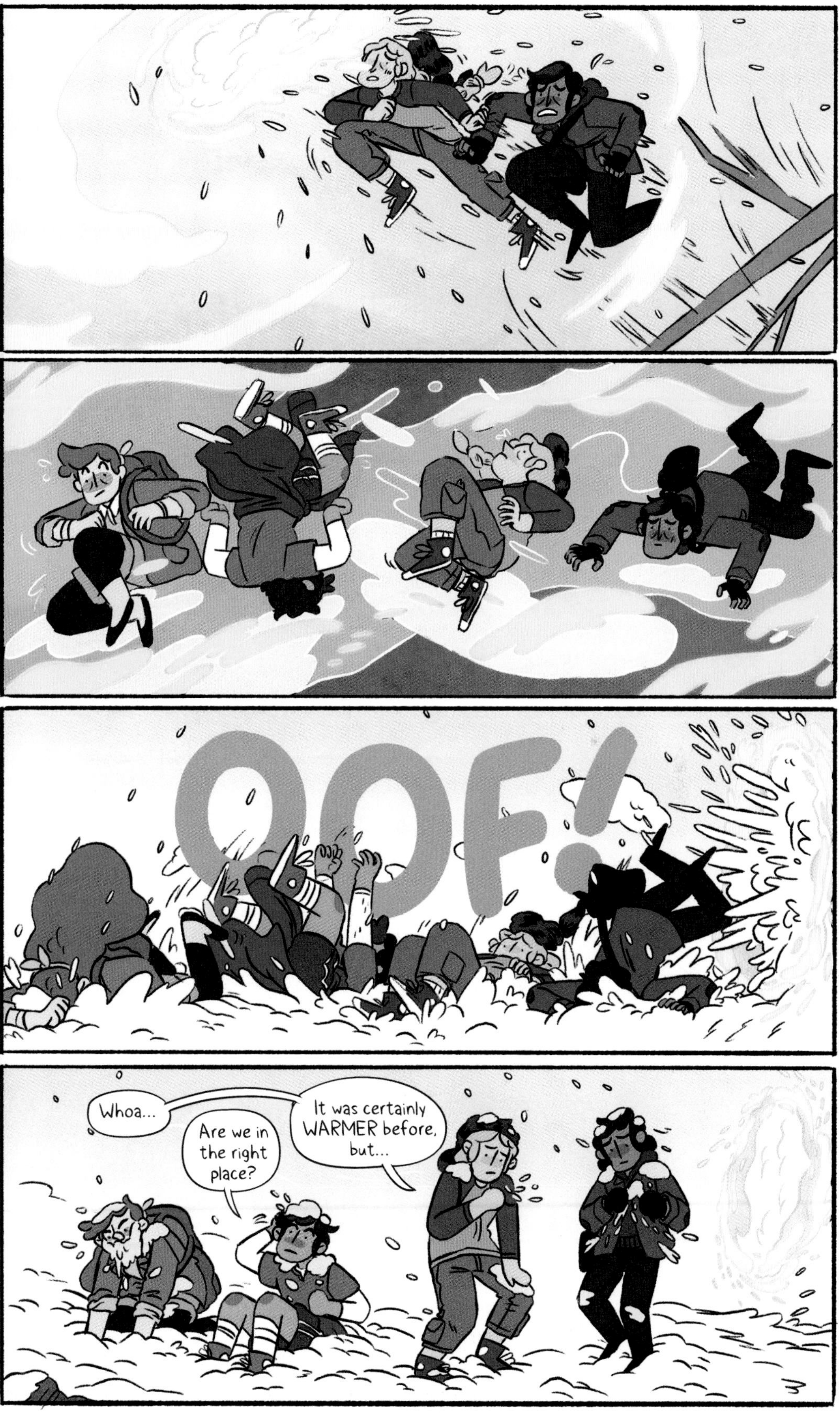
OOF!
Whoa...
Are we in the right place?
It was certainly WARMER before, but...

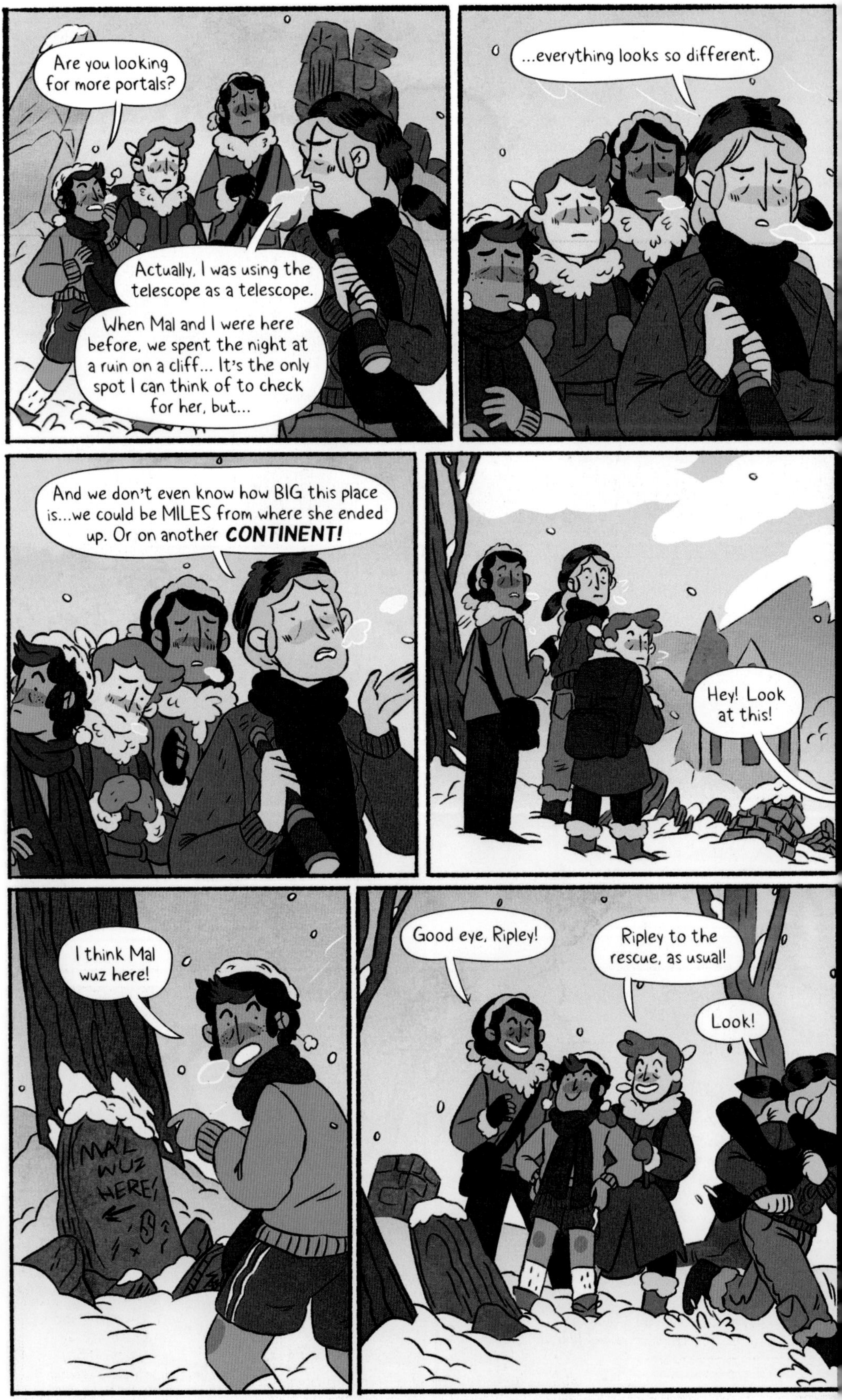
Are you looking for more portals?
Actually, I was using the telescope as a telescope.
When Mal and I were here before, we spent the night at a ruin on a cliff... It's the only spot I can think of to check for her, but...
...everything looks so different.
And we don't even know how BIG this place is...we could be MILES from where she ended up. Or on another **CONTINENT!**
Hey! Look at this!
I think Mal wuz here!
MAL WUZ HERE!
Good eye, Ripley!
Ripley to the rescue, as usual!
Look!

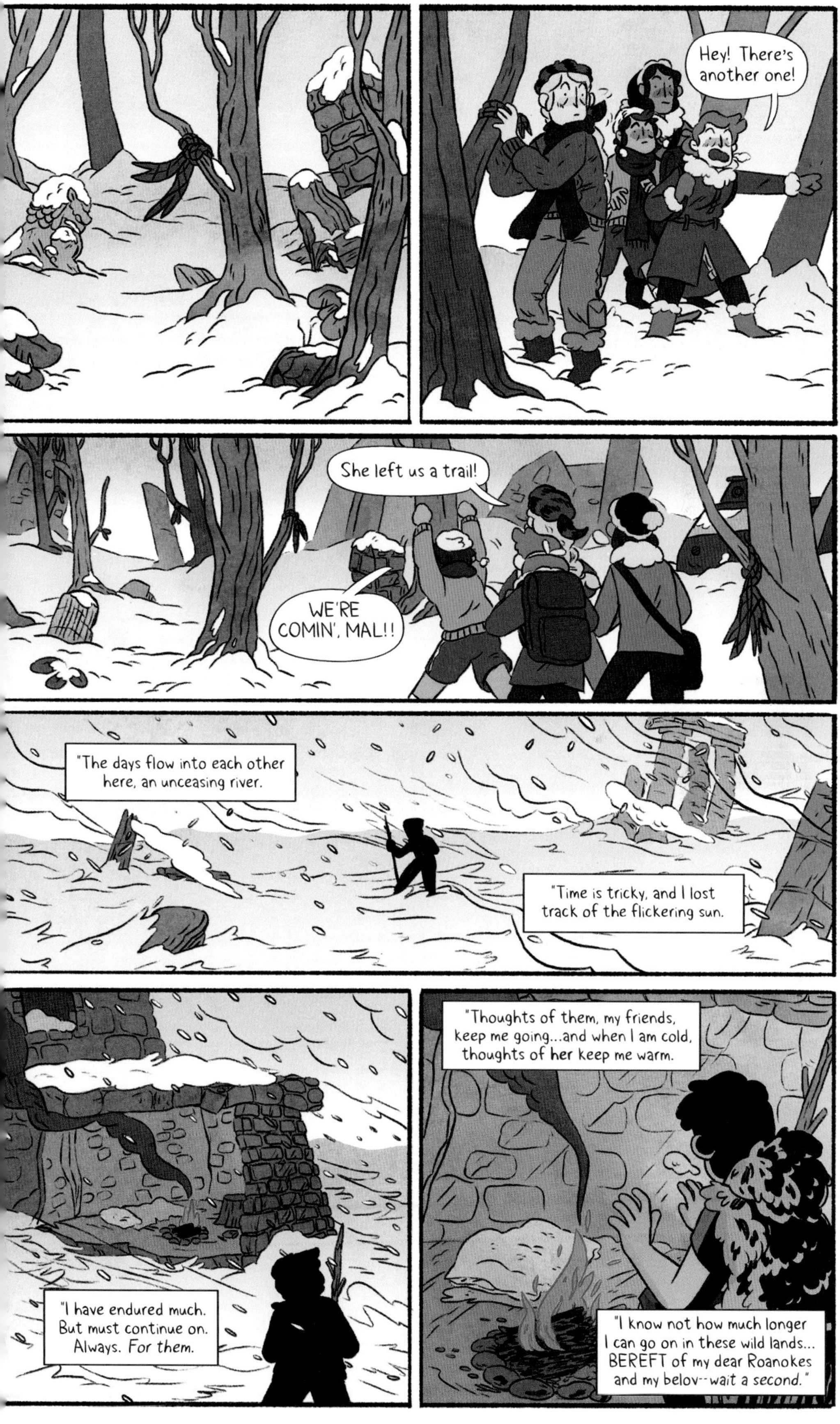
Hey! There's another one!
She left us a trail!
WE'RE COMIN', MAL!!
"The days flow into each other here, an unceasing river.
"Time is tricky, and I lost track of the flickering sun.
"I have endured much. But must continue on. Always. For them.
"Thoughts of them, my friends, keep me going...and when I am cold, thoughts of her keep me warm.
"I know not how much longer I can go on in these wild lands... BEREFT of my dear Roanokes and my belov--wait a second."

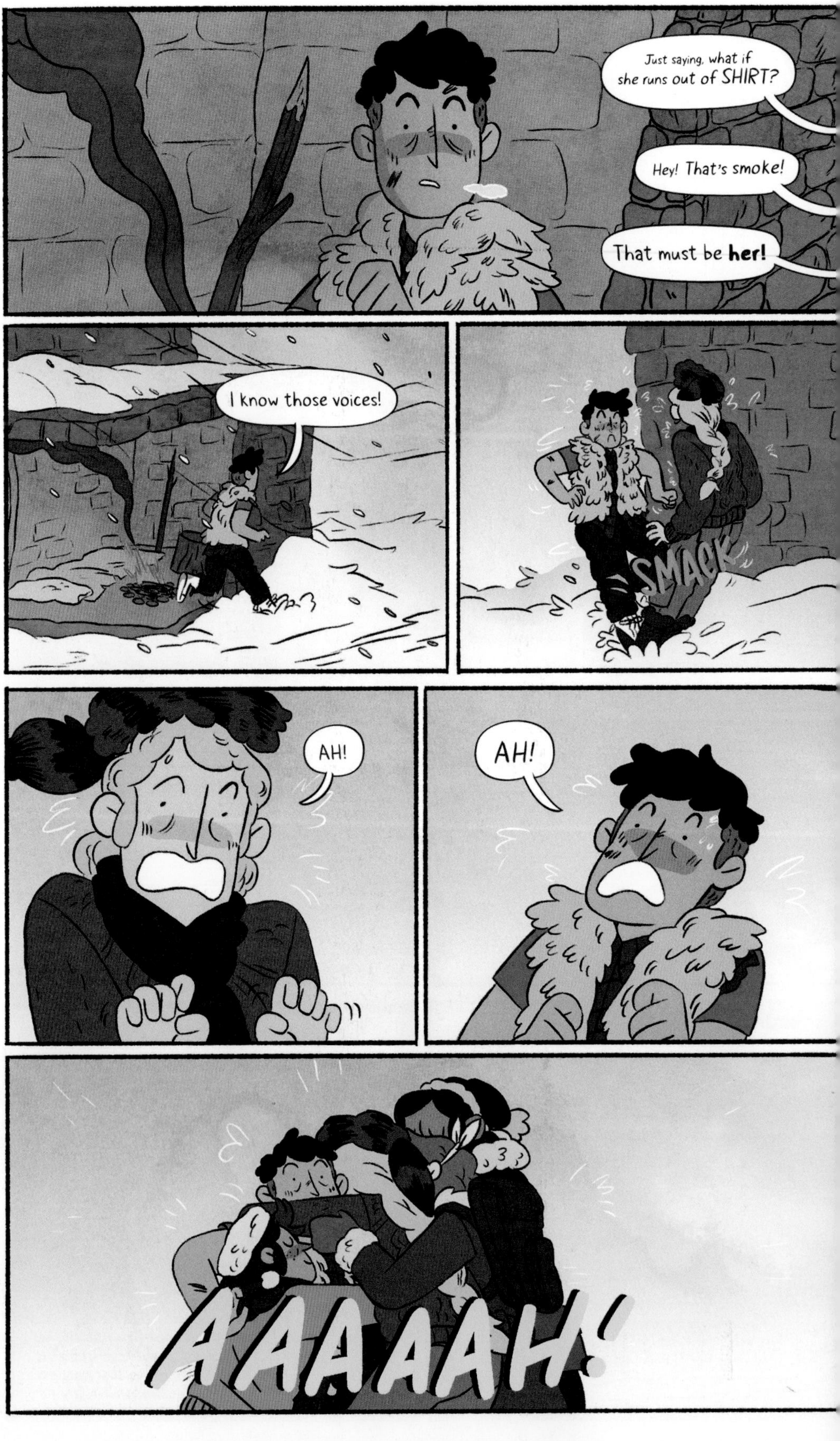

Just saying, what if she runs out of SHIRT?
Hey! That's smoke!
That must be **her!**
I know those voices!
SMACK
AH!
AH!
AAAAAH!

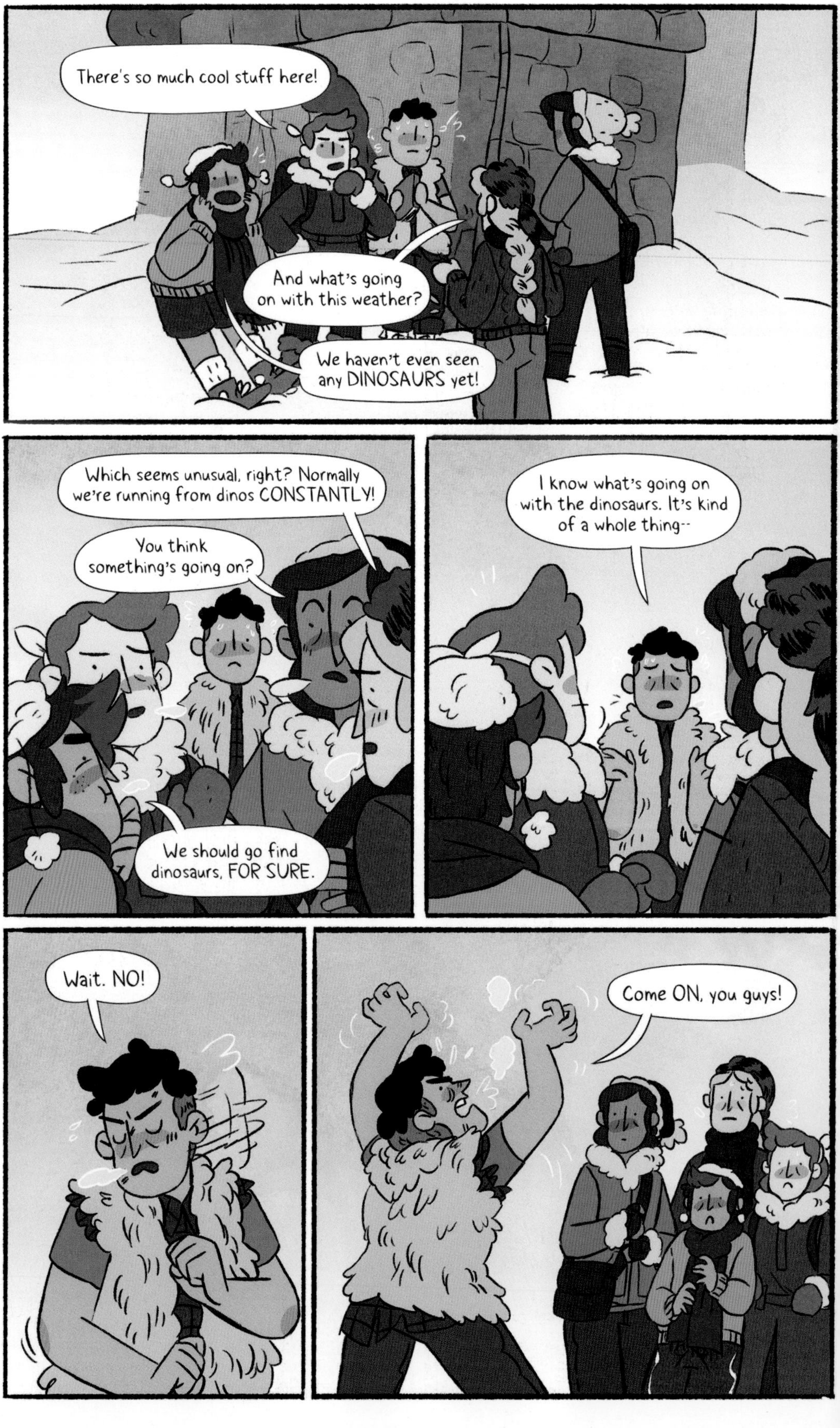
There's so much cool stuff here!
And what's going on with this weather?
We haven't even seen any DINOSAURS yet!
Which seems unusual, right? Normally we're running from dinos CONSTANTLY!
You think something's going on?
We should go find dinosaurs, FOR SURE.
I know what's going on with the dinosaurs. It's kind of a whole thing--
Wait. NO!
Come ON, you guys!

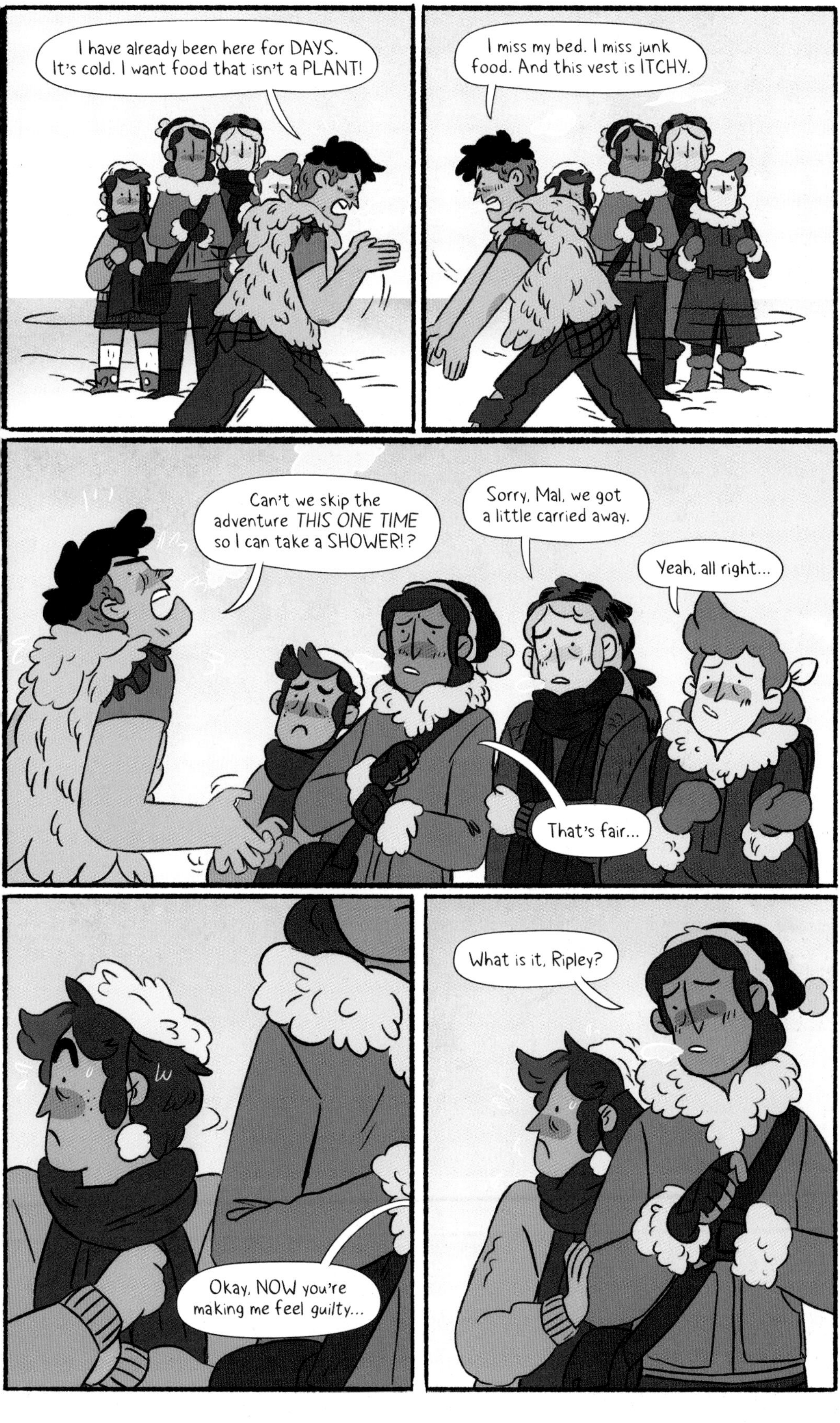
I have already been here for DAYS. It's cold. I want food that isn't a PLANT!
I miss my bed. I miss junk food. And this vest is ITCHY.
Can't we skip the adventure *THIS ONE TIME* so I can take a SHOWER!?
Sorry, Mal, we got a little carried away.
Yeah, all right...
That's fair...
Okay, NOW you're making me feel guilty...
What is it, Ripley?

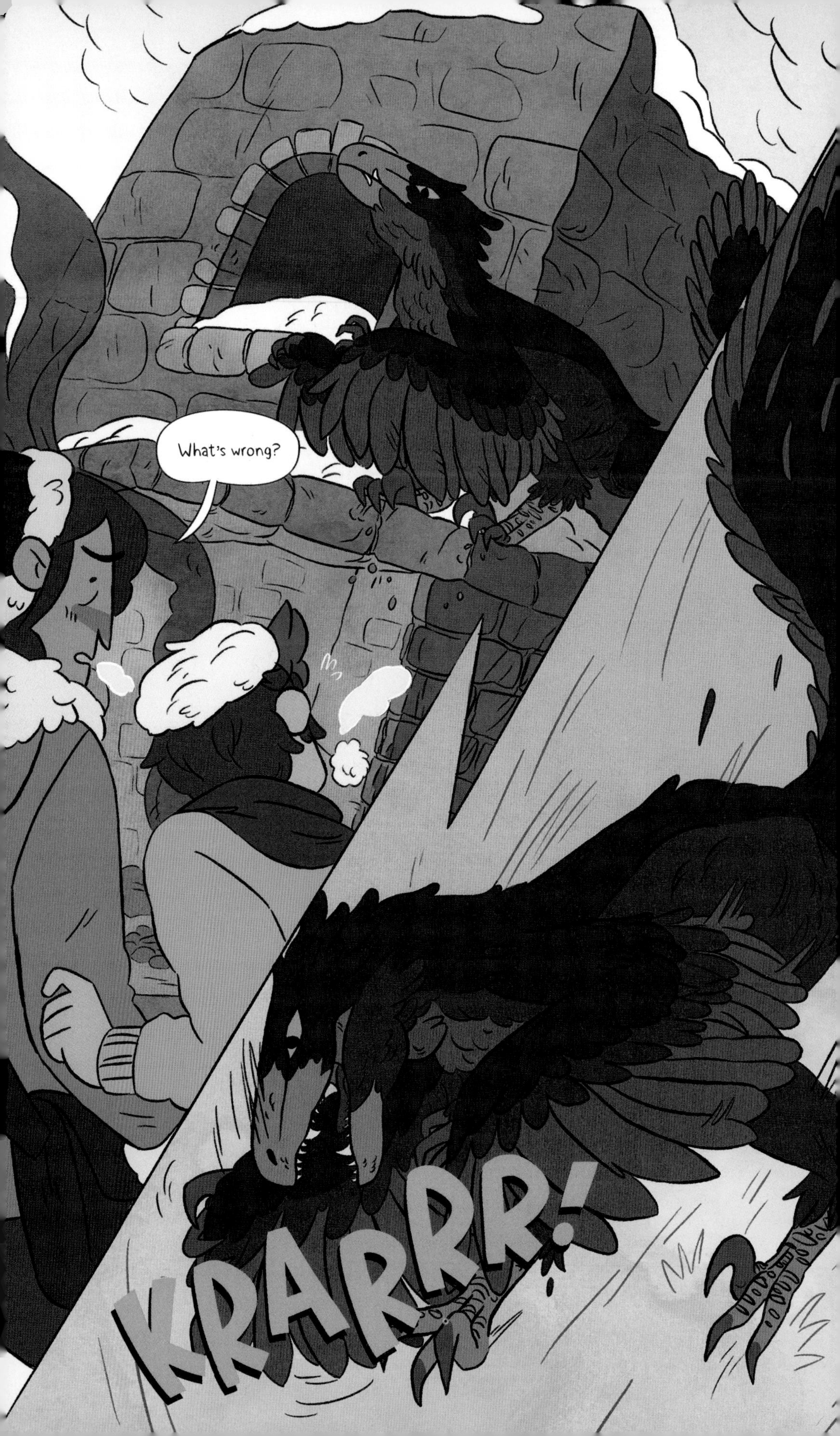
What's wrong?
KRARRR!

will co[...]

The[...]
It helps[...] hould be worn at camp
appearan[...] vents when Lumberjanes
dress fo[...] may also be worn at other
Further[...]ions. It should be worn as a
Lumber[...] the uniform dress with
to have[...]rect shoes, and stocking or
part in[...]
Thiskw[...]ut grows her uniform or
Hardc[...] her Lumberjane.
have [...] sign[...]a she has
thems[...] her
[...] her

The[...]
yellow, [...]
emb[...]
the w[...]
choos[...]
slacks, [...]
made o[...]
out-of-do[...]
green bere[...]
the colla[...]
Shoes may b[...]
heels, round[...] ings or
socks should[...] the shoes or wi[...]
the uniform. Ne[...]s, bracelets, or other jewelry do [...]
belong with a Lumberjane uniform.

IT'S GOTTA BE
HERE SOMEWHE[...]

IT'S ALWAYS IN THE
LAST PLACE YOU LOOK...

HOW TO WEAR THE UNIFORM

To look well in a uniform demands first of [...]
uniform be kept in good condition—clean [...]
pressed. See that the skirt is the right length for your own
height and build, that the belt is adjusted to your waist,
that your shoes and stockings are in keeping with the
uniform, that you watch your posture and carry yourself
with dignity and grace. If the beret is removed indoors,
be sure that your hair is neat and kept in place with an
inconspicuous clip or ribbon. When you wear a
Lumberjane uniform you are identified as a member of
this organization and you should be doubly careful to
conduct yourself in a way that will show everyone that
courtesy and thoughtfulness are part of being a
Lumberjane. People are likely to judge a whole nation by
the selfishness of a few individuals, to criticize a whole
family because of the misconduct of one member, and to
feel unkindly toward an organization because of the

The unifor[...]
helps to cre[...]
in a group. [...]
active life th[...]
another bond[...]
future, and pr[...]
in order to b[...]
Lumberjane pr[...]
Penniquiqul Thi[...]re Lady
Types, but m[...]s will wish to have one. They
can either bu[...]e uniform, or make it themselves from
materials available at the trading post.

WHY CAN'T WE
LOOK THERE FIRST?!

LUMBERJANES FIELD MANUAL

CHAPTER
SIXTY-THREE

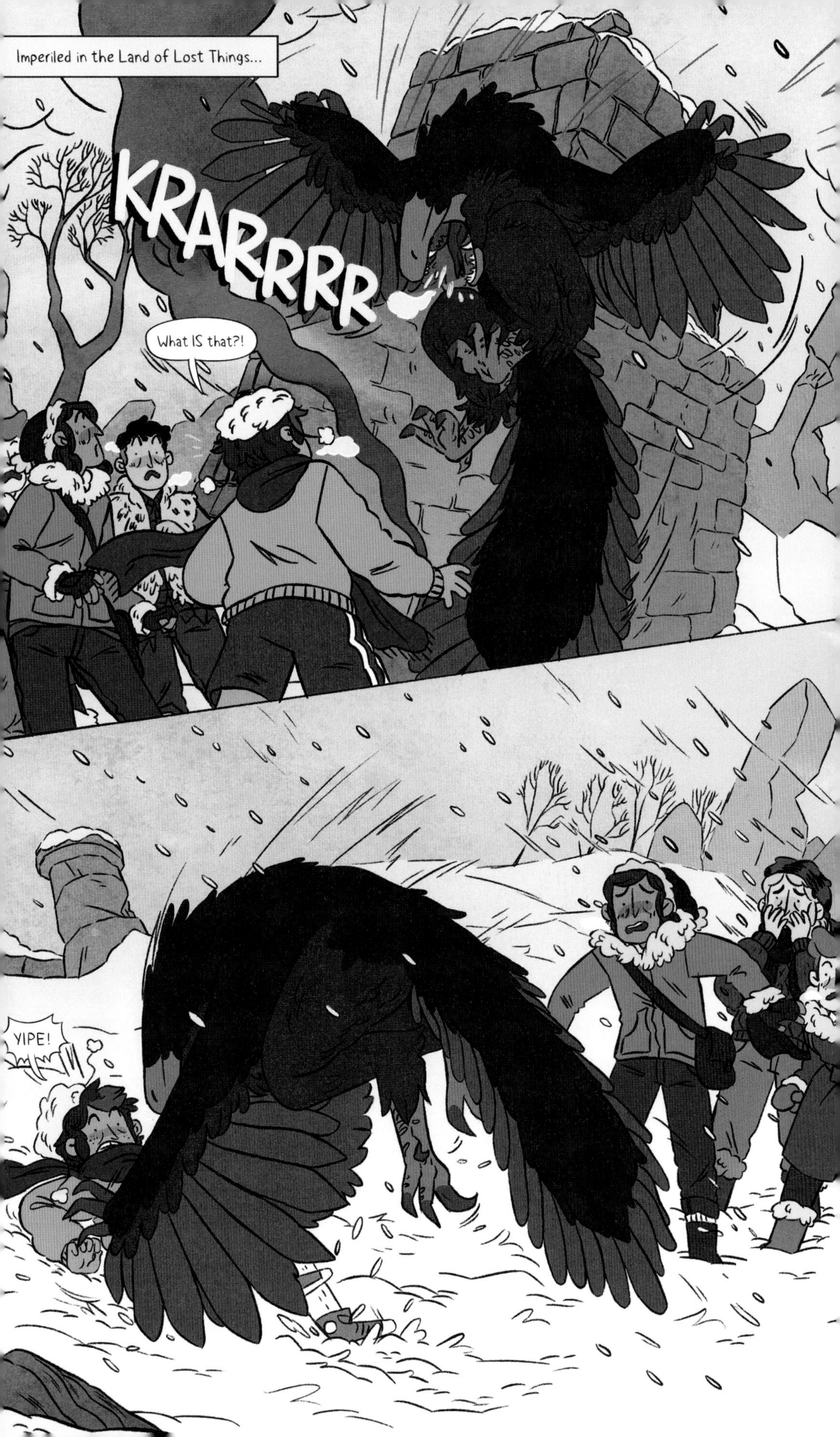
Imperiled in the Land of Lost Things...
KRARRRRR
What IS that?!
YIPE!

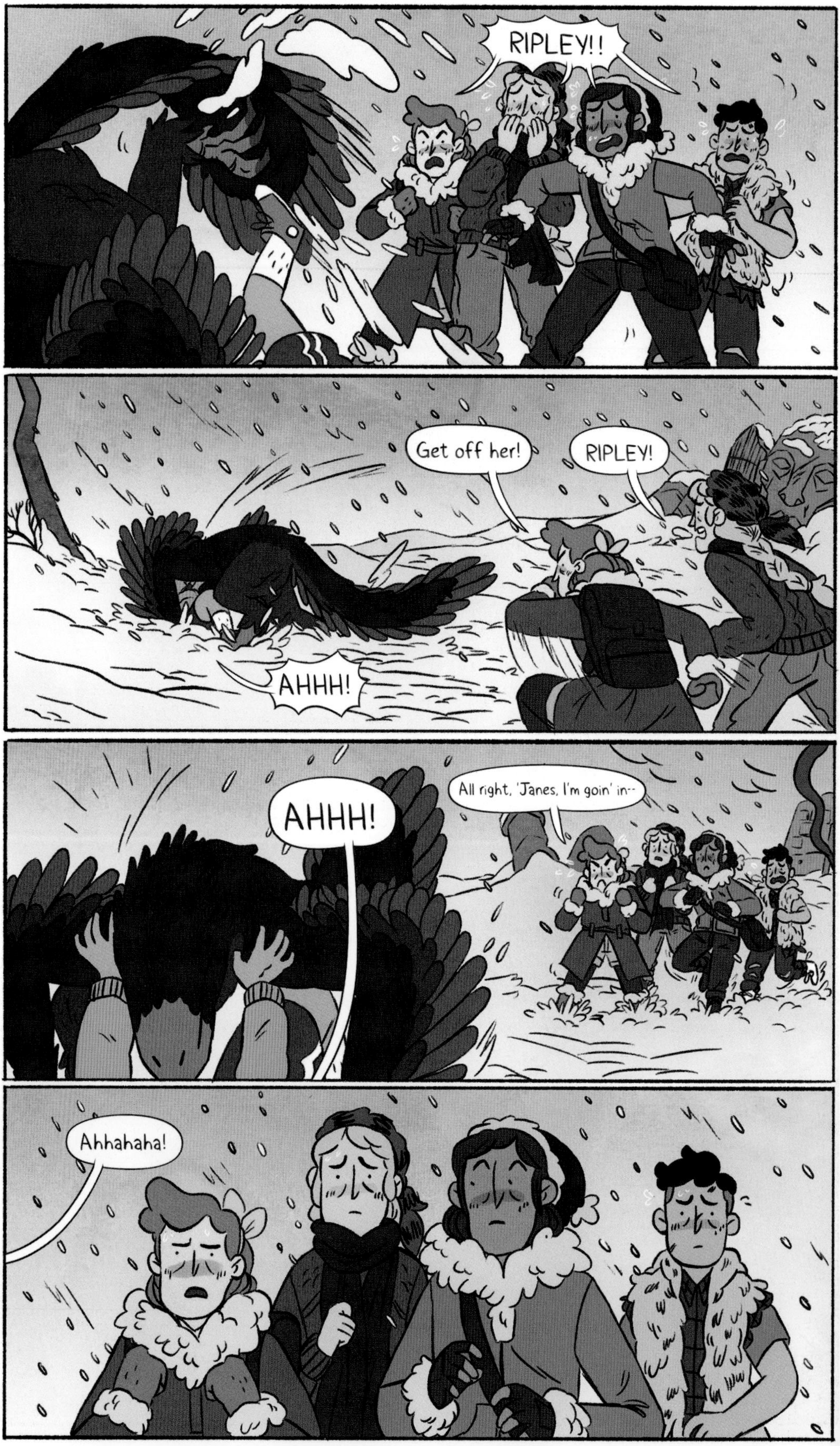
RIPLEY!!
Get off her!
RIPLEY!
AHHH!
AHHH!
All right, 'Janes, I'm goin' in--
Ahhahaha!

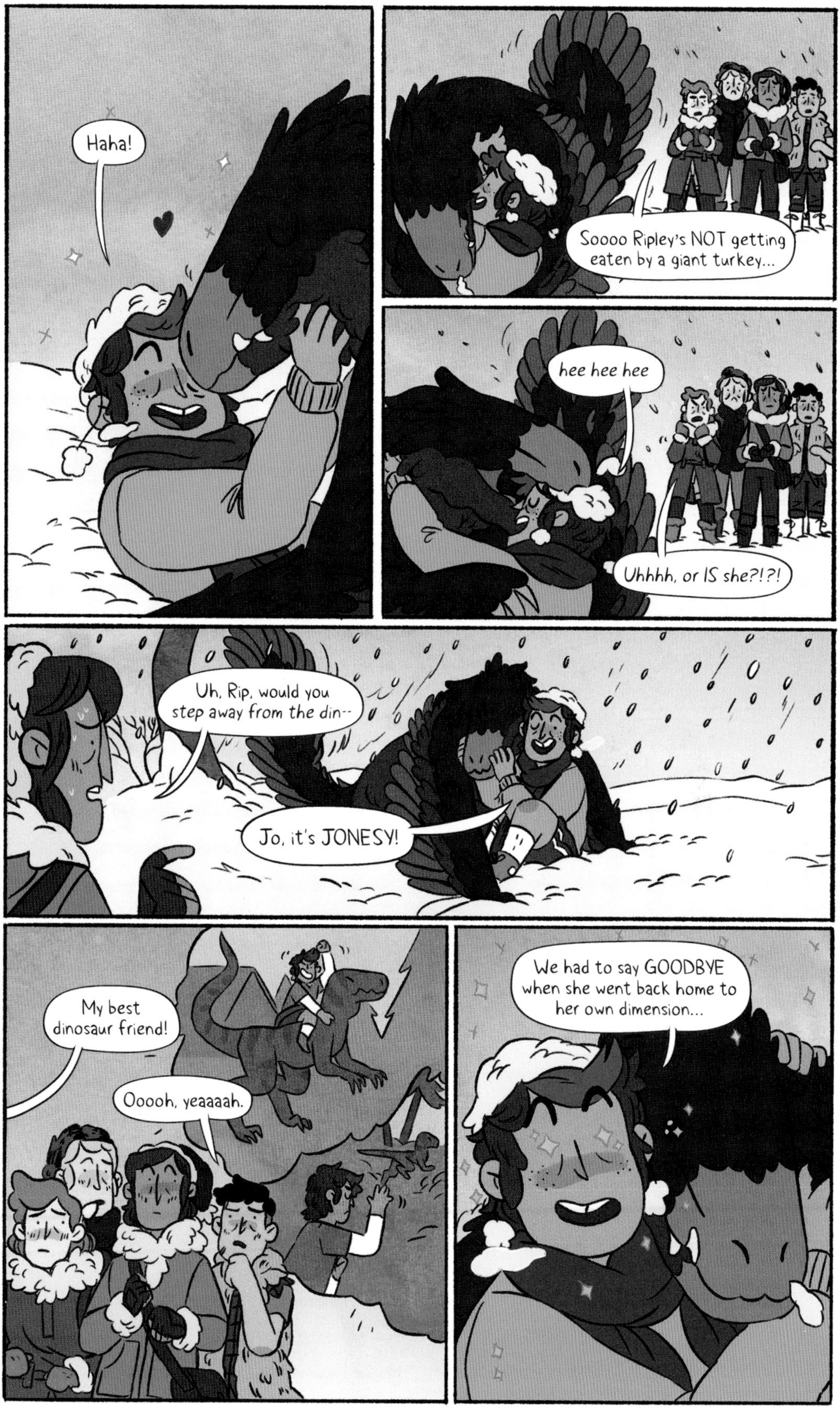
Haha!
Soooo Ripley's NOT getting eaten by a giant turkey...
hee hee hee
Uhhhh, or IS she?!?!
Uh, Rip, would you step away from the din--
Jo, it's JONESY!
My best dinosaur friend!
Ooooh, yeaaaah.
We had to say GOODBYE when she went back home to her own dimension...

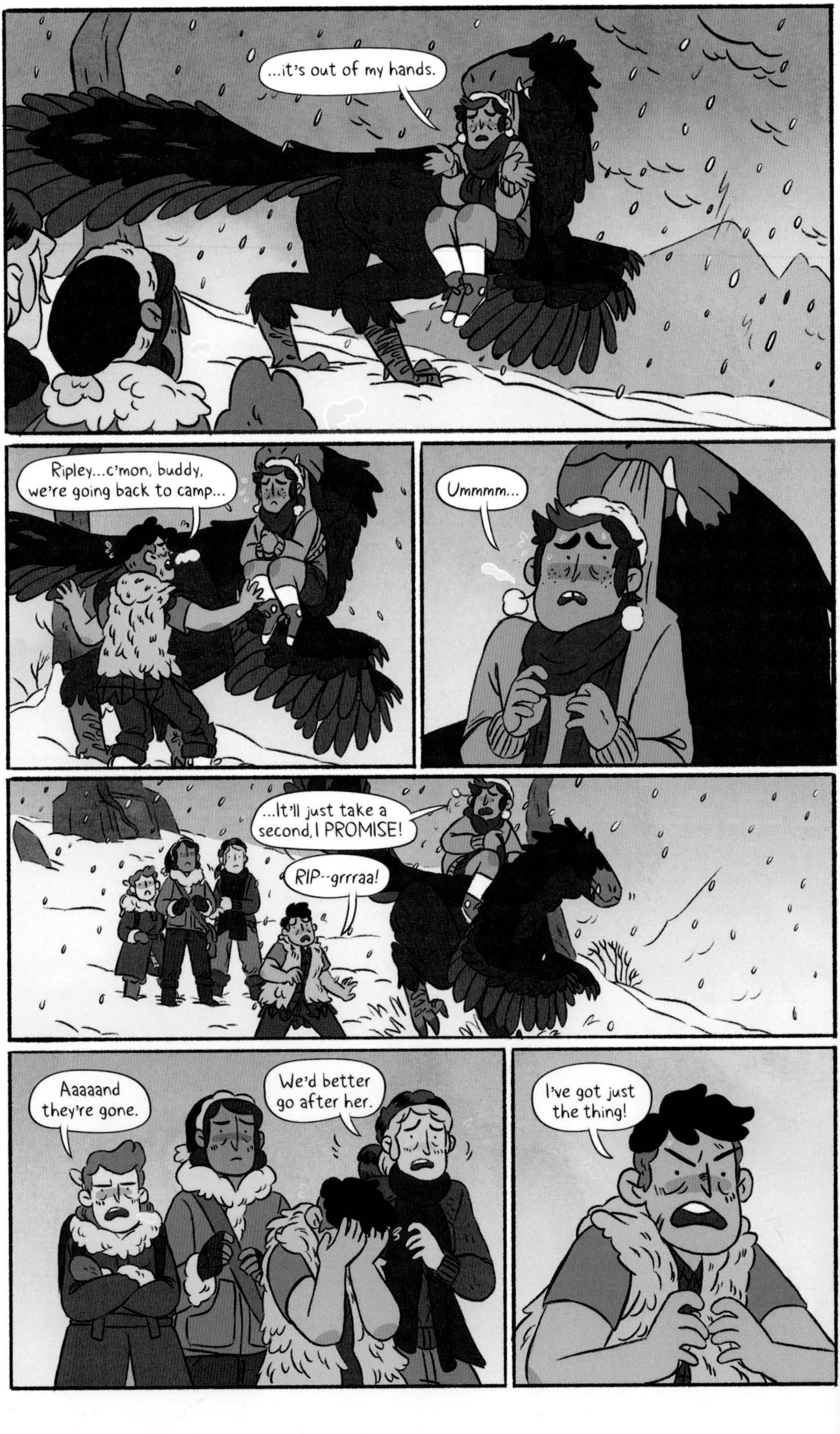
...it's out of my hands.
Ripley...c'mon, buddy, we're going back to camp...
Ummmm...
...It'll just take a second, I PROMISE!
RIP--grrraa!
Aaaaand they're gone.
We'd better go after her.
I've got just the thing!

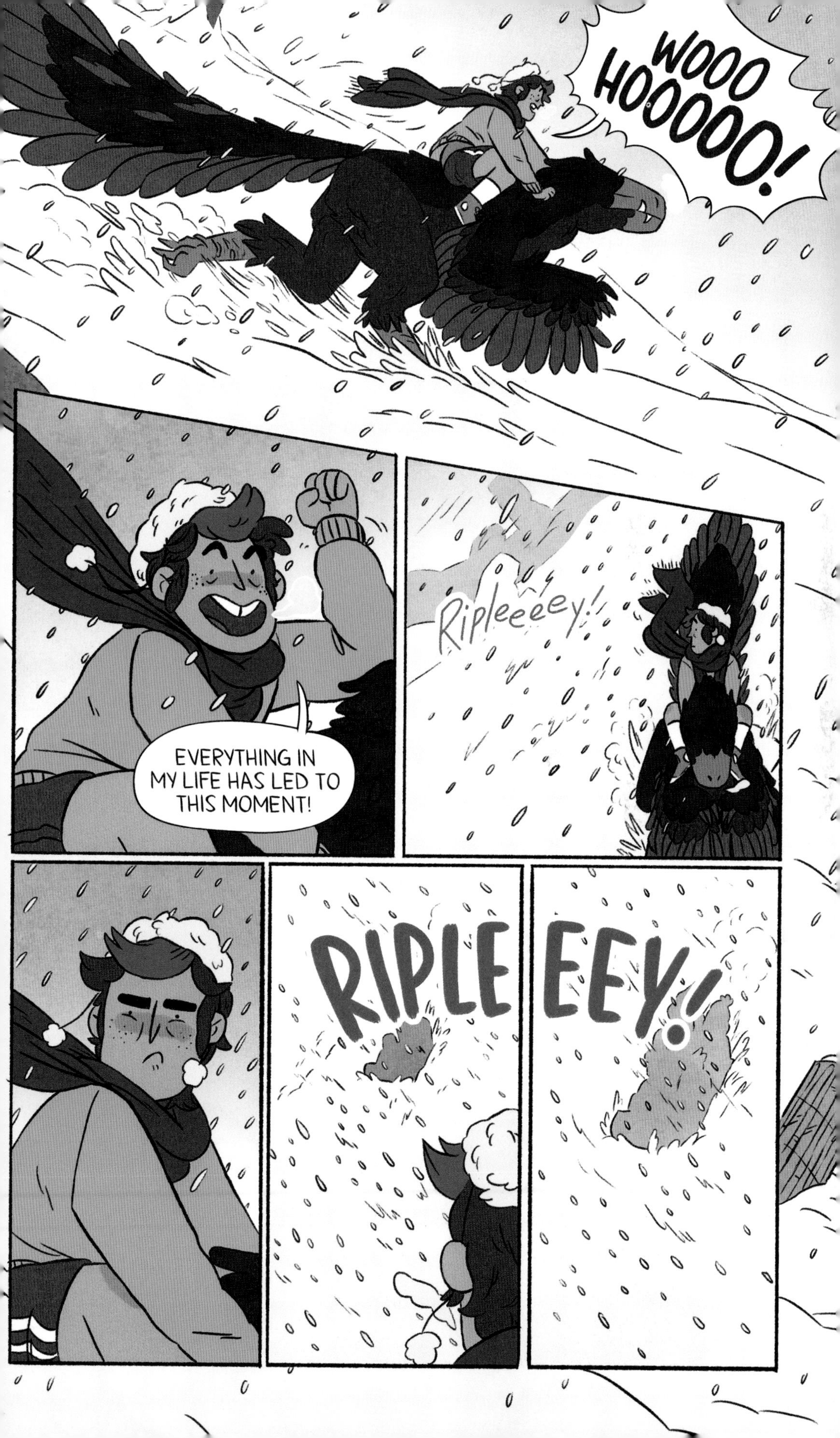
WOOO HOOOOOO!
EVERYTHING IN MY LIFE HAS LED TO THIS MOMENT!
Ripleeeey!
RIPLEEY!

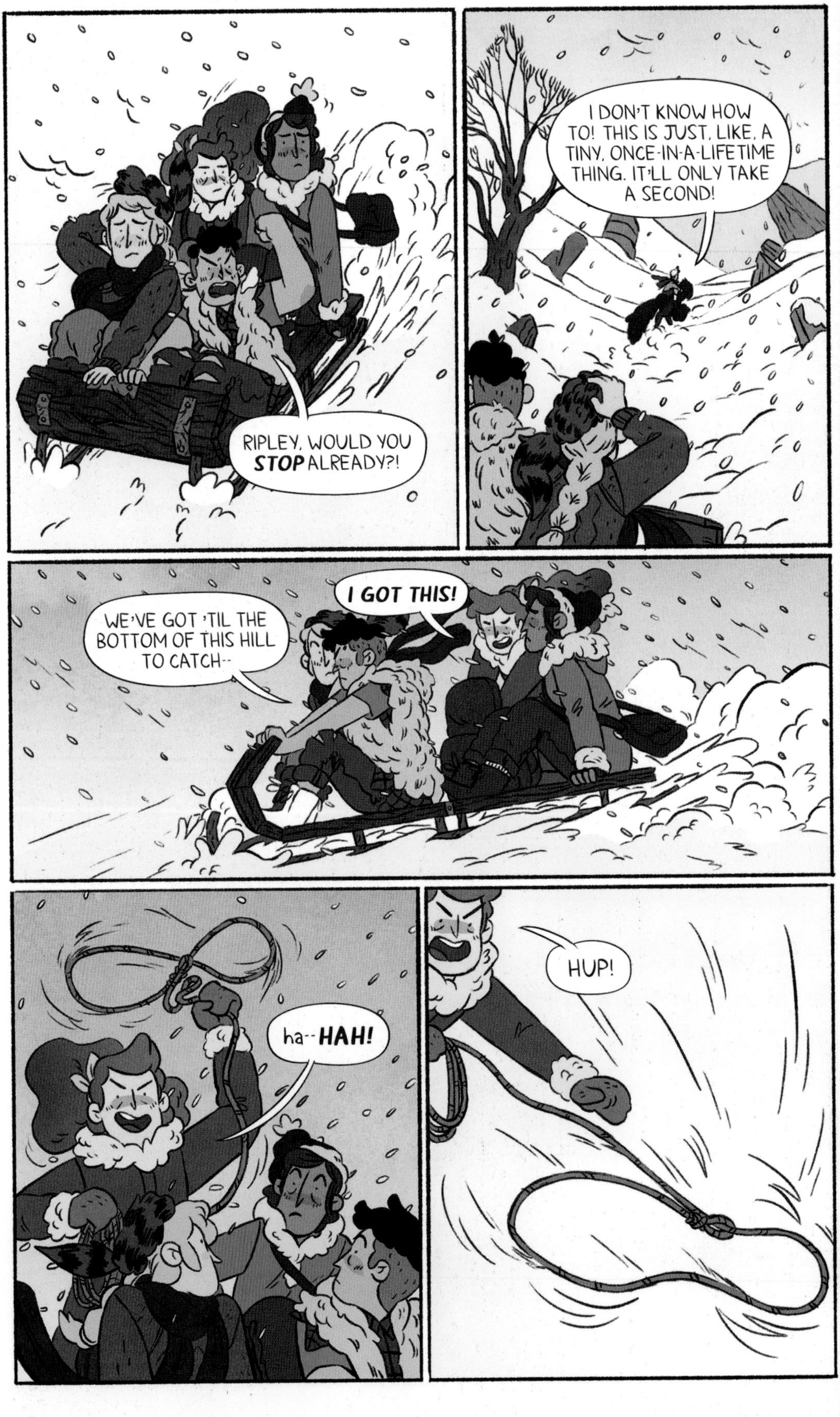

RIPLEY, WOULD YOU **STOP** ALREADY?!
I DON'T KNOW HOW TO! THIS IS JUST, LIKE, A TINY, ONCE-IN-A-LIFETIME THING. IT'LL ONLY TAKE A SECOND!
WE'VE GOT 'TIL THE BOTTOM OF THIS HILL TO CATCH--
I GOT THIS!
ha--**HAH!**
HUP!

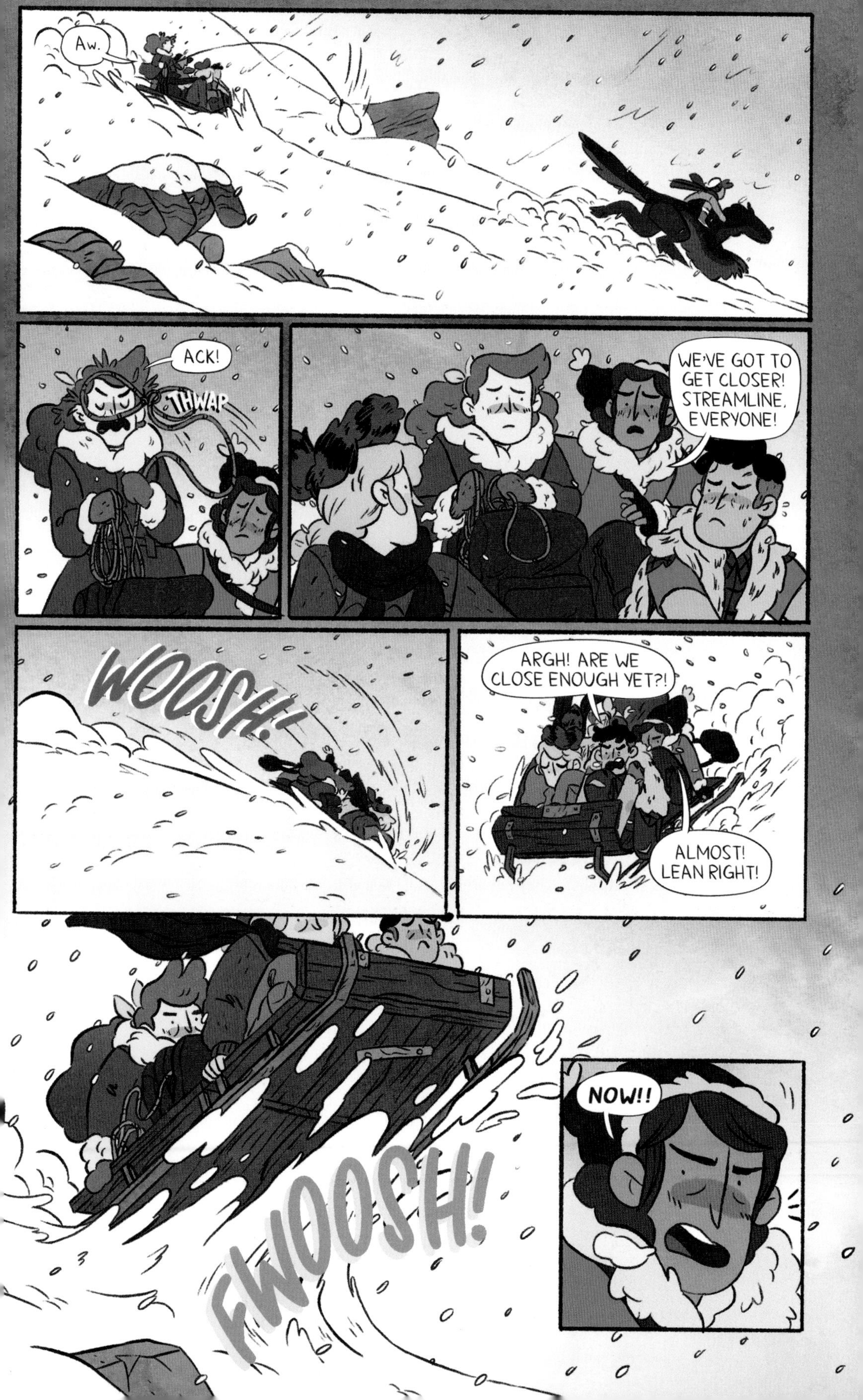

Aw.
ACK!
THWAP
WE'VE GOT TO GET CLOSER! STREAMLINE, EVERYONE!
WOOSH!
ARGH! ARE WE CLOSE ENOUGH YET?!
ALMOST! LEAN RIGHT!
FWOOSH!
NOW!!

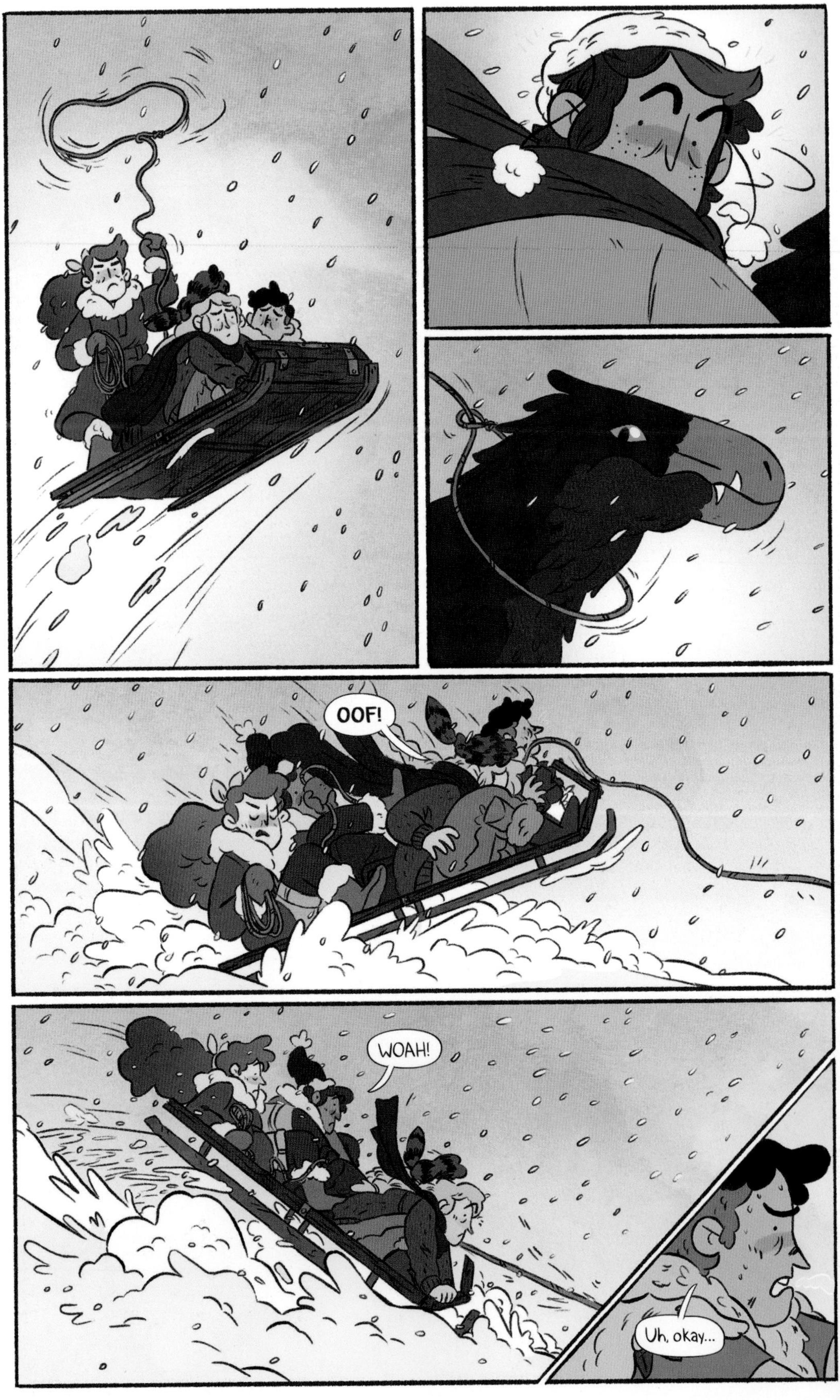
OOF!
WOAH!
Uh, okay...

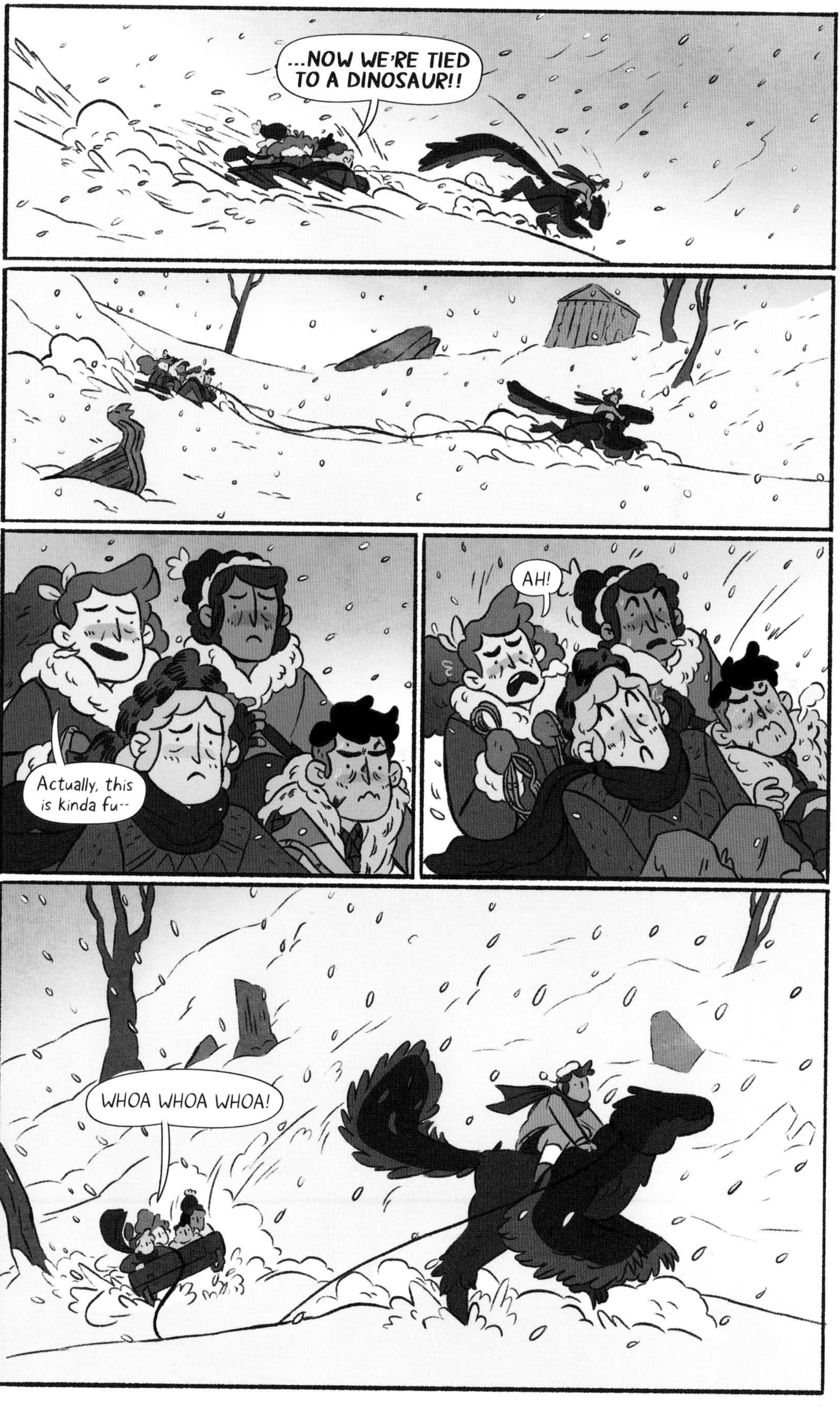
...NOW WE'RE TIED TO A DINOSAUR!!
Actually, this is kinda fu--
AH!
WHOA WHOA WHOA!

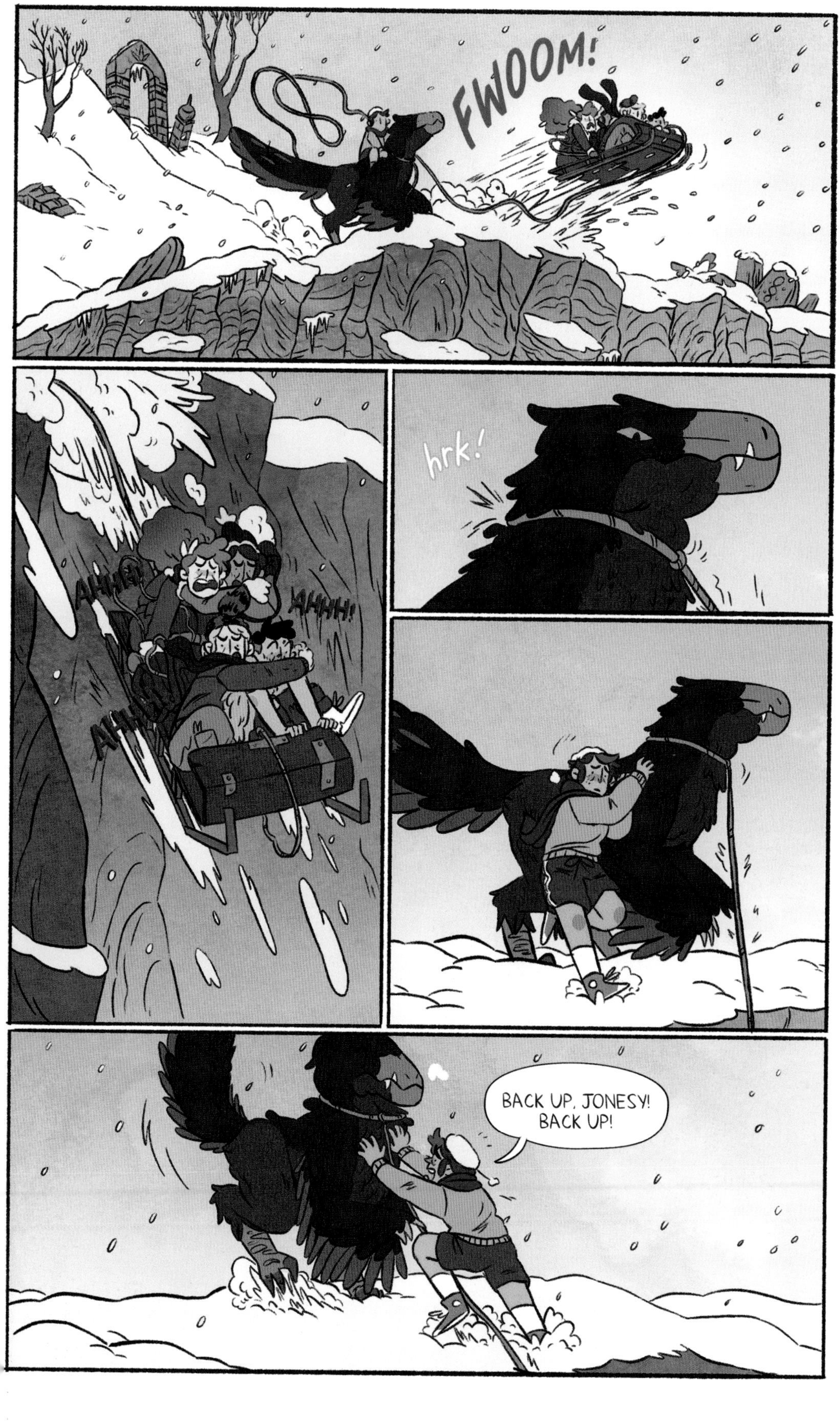
FWOOM!
AHHH!
AHHH!
hrk!
BACK UP, JONESY! BACK UP!

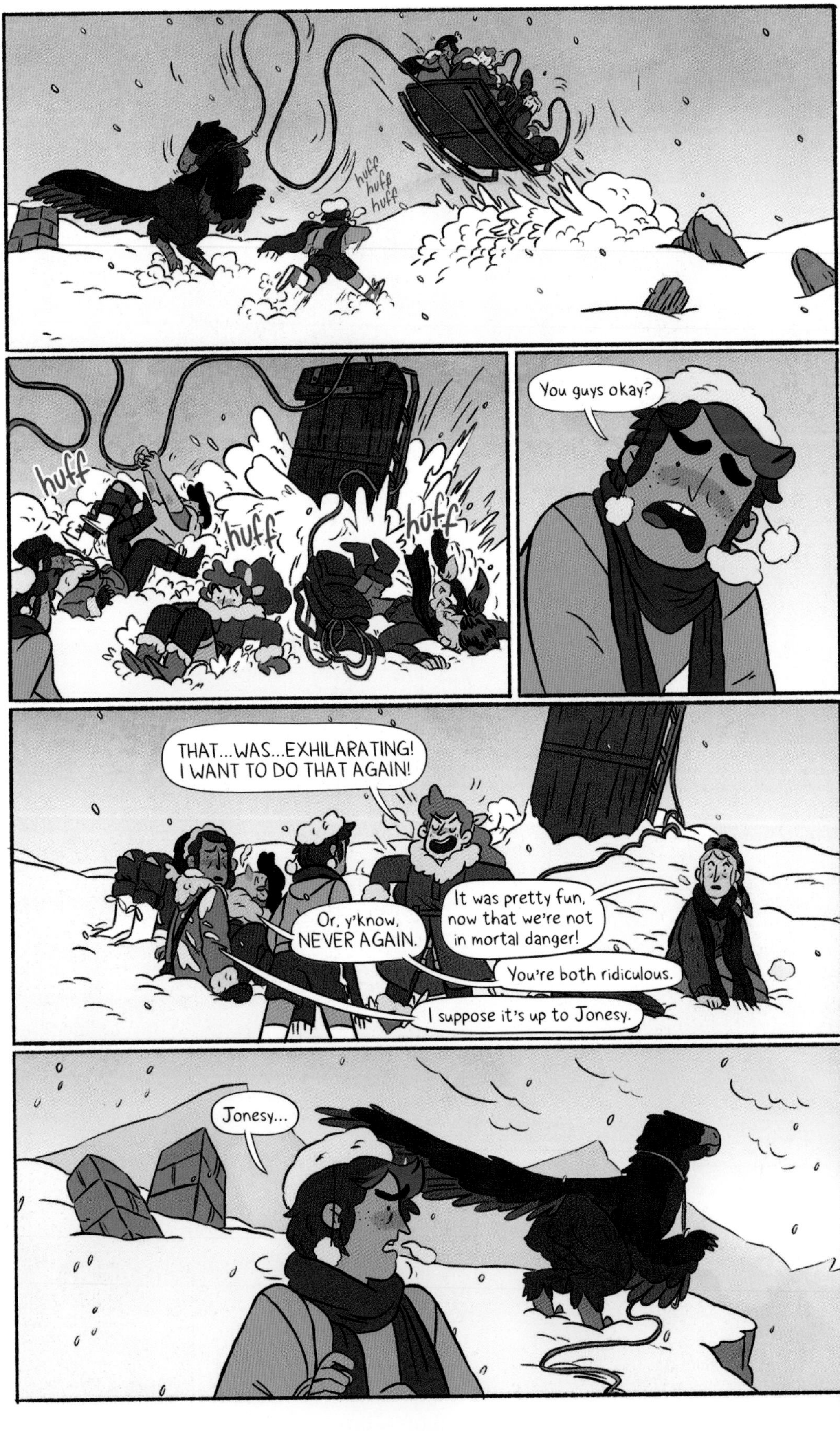
huff
huff
huff
huff
huff
huff
You guys okay?
THAT...WAS...EXHILARATING! I WANT TO DO THAT AGAIN!
It was pretty fun, now that we're not in mortal danger!
Or, y'know, NEVER AGAIN.
You're both ridiculous.
I suppose it's up to Jonesy.
Jonesy...

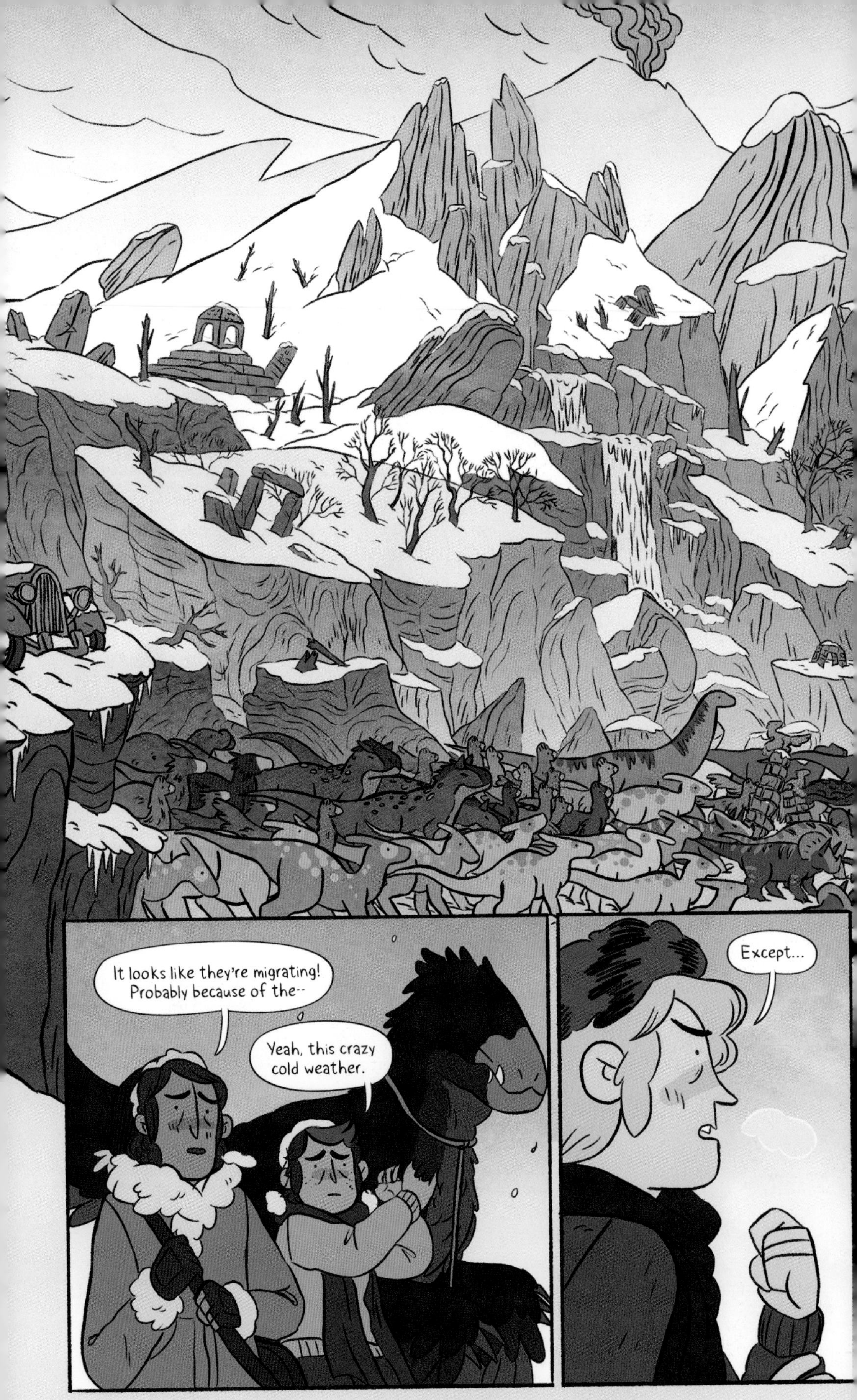
It looks like they're migrating! Probably because of the--
Yeah, this crazy cold weather.
Except...

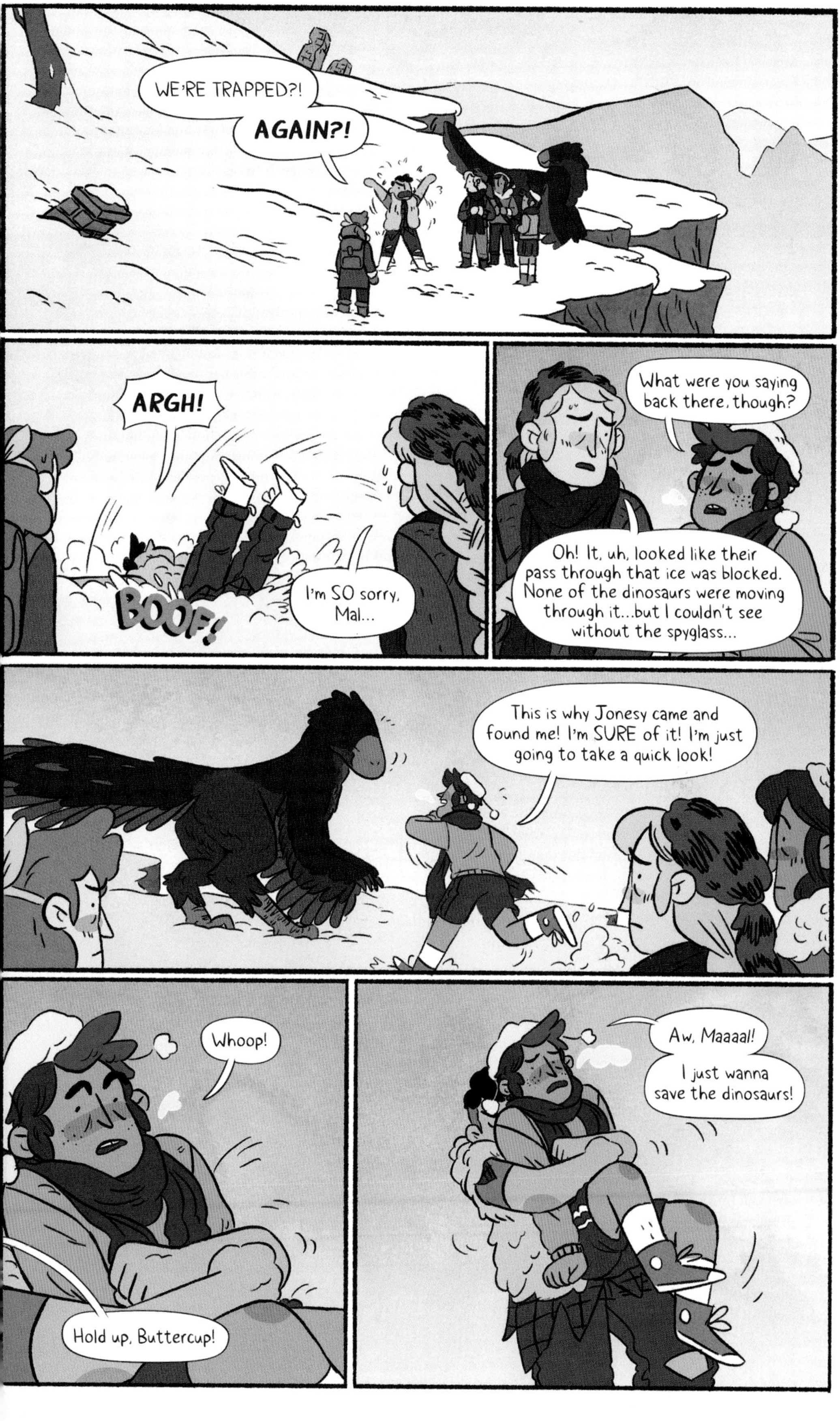
WE'RE TRAPPED?!
AGAIN?!
ARGH!
BOOF!
I'm SO sorry, Mal...
What were you saying back there, though?
Oh! It, uh, looked like their pass through that ice was blocked. None of the dinosaurs were moving through it...but I couldn't see without the spyglass...
This is why Jonesy came and found me! I'm SURE of it! I'm just going to take a quick look!
Whoop!
Hold up, Buttercup!
Aw, Maaaal!
I just wanna save the dinosaurs!

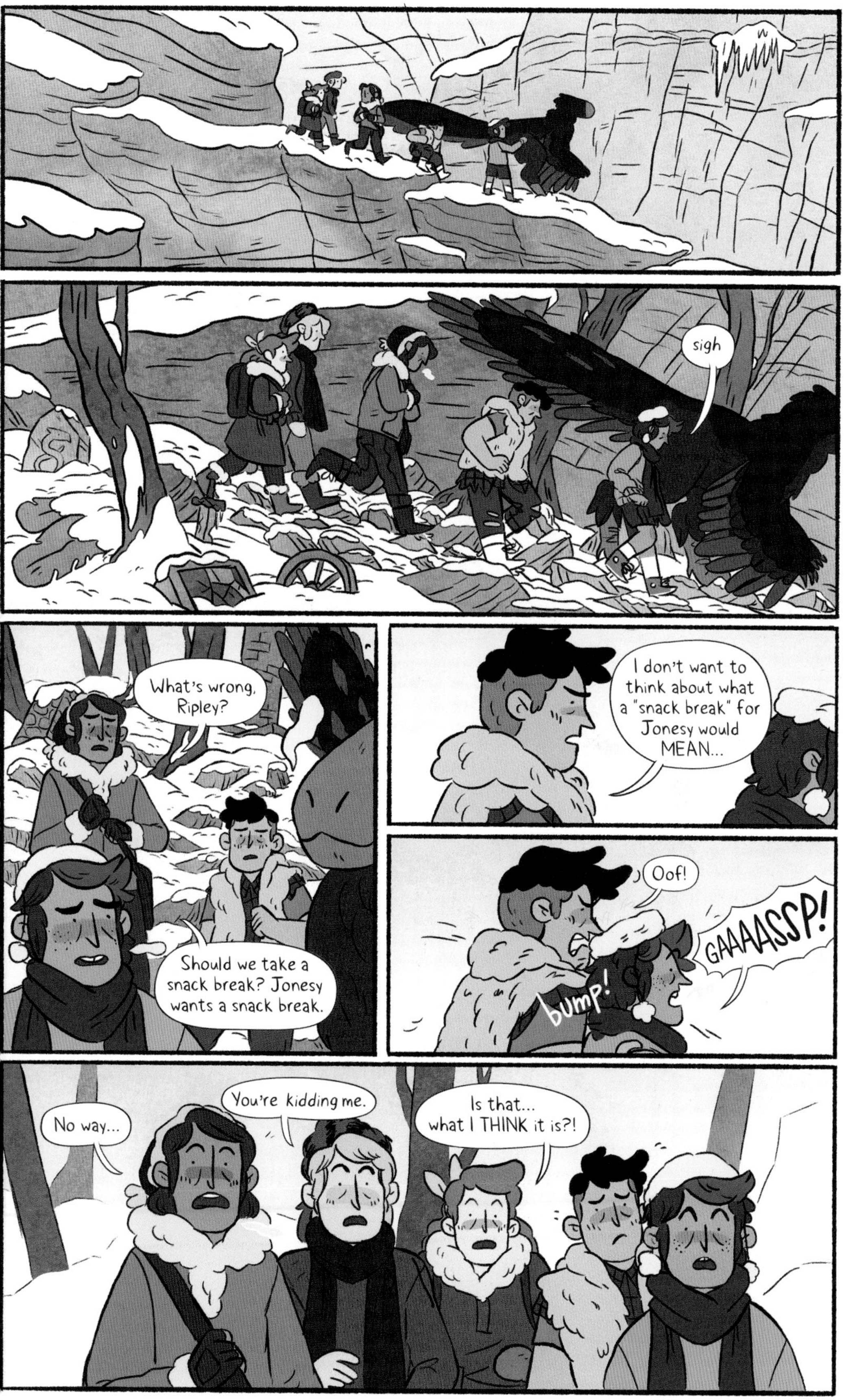

sigh
What's wrong, Ripley?
Should we take a snack break? Jonesy wants a snack break.
I don't want to think about what a "snack break" for Jonesy would MEAN...
Oof!
GAAAASSP!
bump!
No way...
You're kidding me.
Is that... what I THINK it is?!

will co...

The...
It helps...
appearan...
dress fo...
Further...
Lumber...
to have...
part in...
Thiskv...
Hardo...
have...
them...

THE UNIFORM

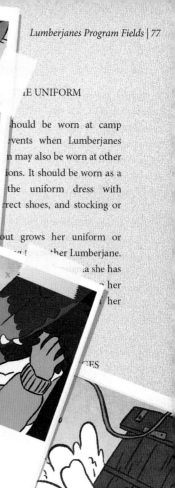

...should be worn at camp ...events when Lumberjanes ...n may also be worn at other ...ions. It should be worn as a ...the uniform dress with ...rrect shoes, and stocking or ...out grows her uniform or ...her Lumberjane. ...signa she has ...her ...her

The...
yellow, short sl... emb... the w... choose... slacks, made o... out-of-do... green bere... the colla... Shoes ma b... heels, round... socks should... with the shoes or wi... the uniform. Ne... es, bracelets, or other jewelry do... belong with a Lumberjane uniform.

HOW TO WEAR THE UNIFORM

To look well in a uniform demands first of... uniform be kept in good condition—clean... pressed. See that the skirt is the right length for your own height and build, that the belt is adjusted to your waist, that your shoes and stockings are in keeping with the uniform, that you watch your posture and carry yourself with dignity and grace. If the beret is removed indoors, be sure that your hair is neat and kept in place with an inconspicuous clip or ribbon. When you wear a Lumberjane uniform you are identified as a member of this organization and you should be doubly careful to conduct yourself in a way that will show everyone that courtesy and thoughtfulness are part of being a Lumberjane. People are likely to judge a whole nation by the selfishness of a few individuals, to criticize a whole family because of the misconduct of one member, and to feel unkindly toward an organization because of the

The unifor... helps to cre... in a group. ... active life th... another bond... future, and pr... in order to b... Lumberjane pr... Penniquiqul Thi... ...ore Lady Types, but m... ...es will wish to have one. They can either bu... the uniform, or make it themselves from materials available at the trading post.

LUMBERJANES FIELD MANUAL

CHAPTER
SIXTY-FOUR

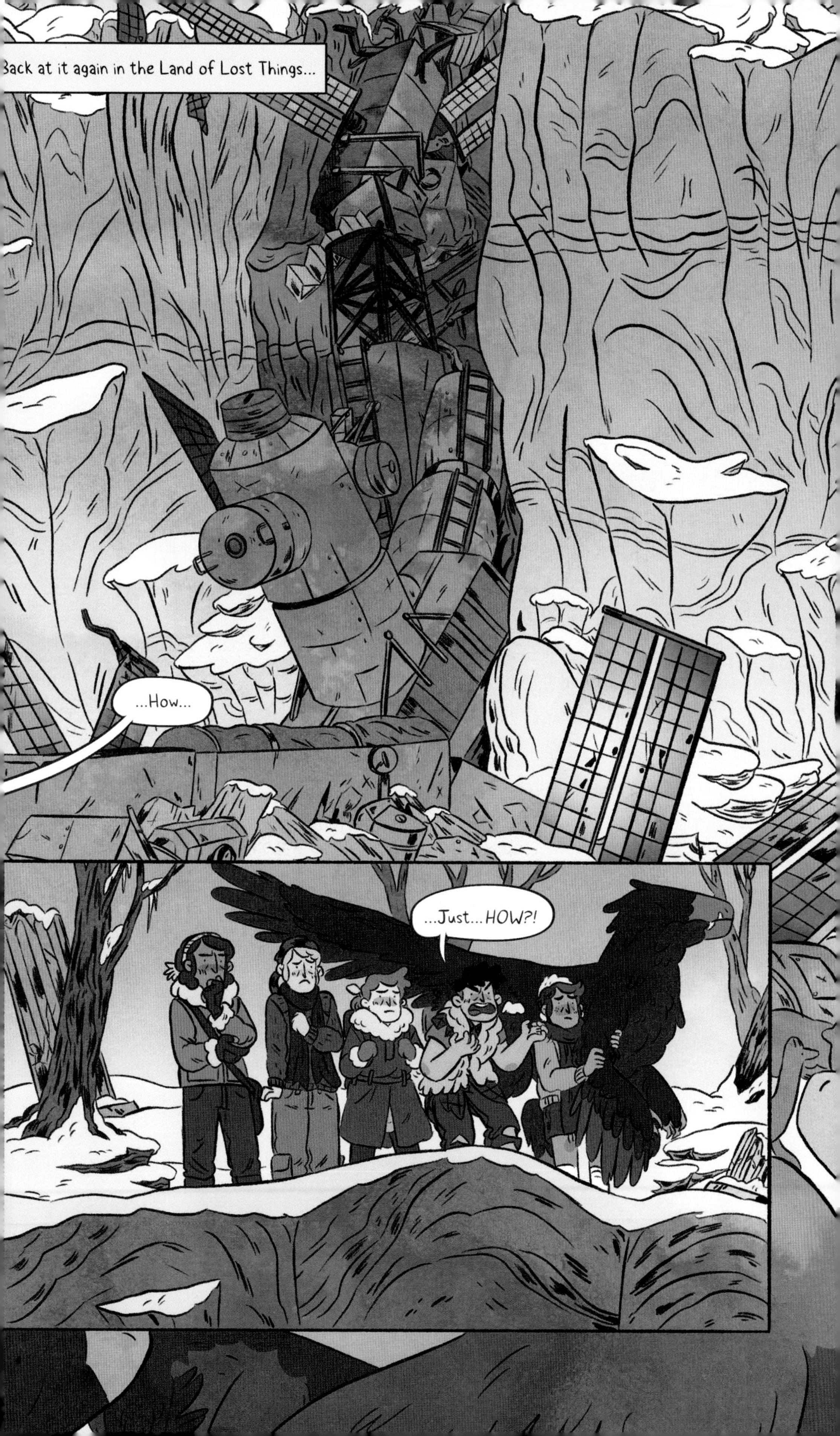
Back at it again in the Land of Lost Things...
...How...
...Just... HOW?!

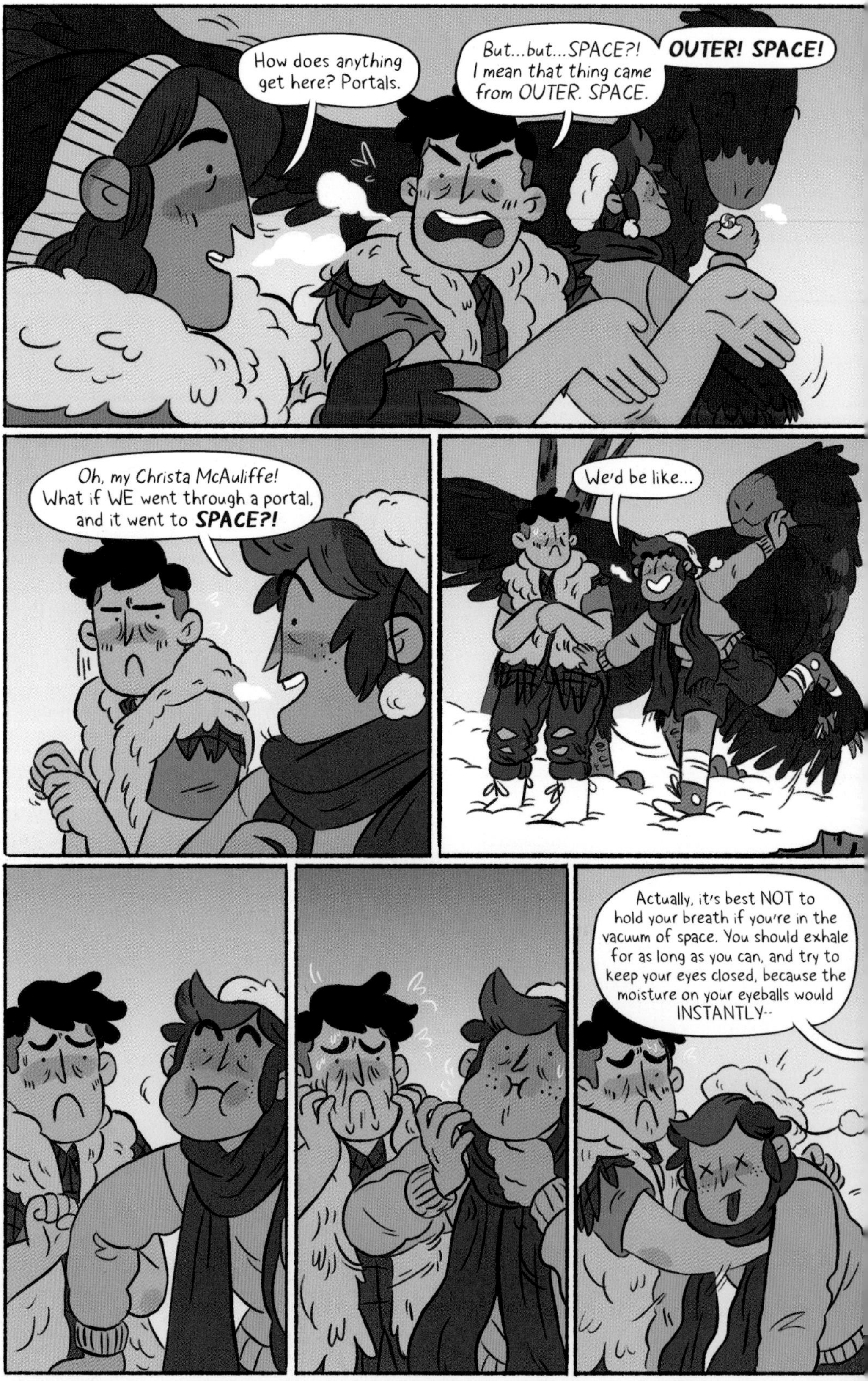
How does anything get here? Portals.
But...but...SPACE?! I mean that thing came from OUTER. SPACE.
OUTER! SPACE!
Oh, my Christa McAuliffe! What if WE went through a portal, and it went to SPACE?!
We'd be like...
Actually, it's best NOT to hold your breath if you're in the vacuum of space. You should exhale for as long as you can, and try to keep your eyes closed, because the moisture on your eyeballs would INSTANTLY--

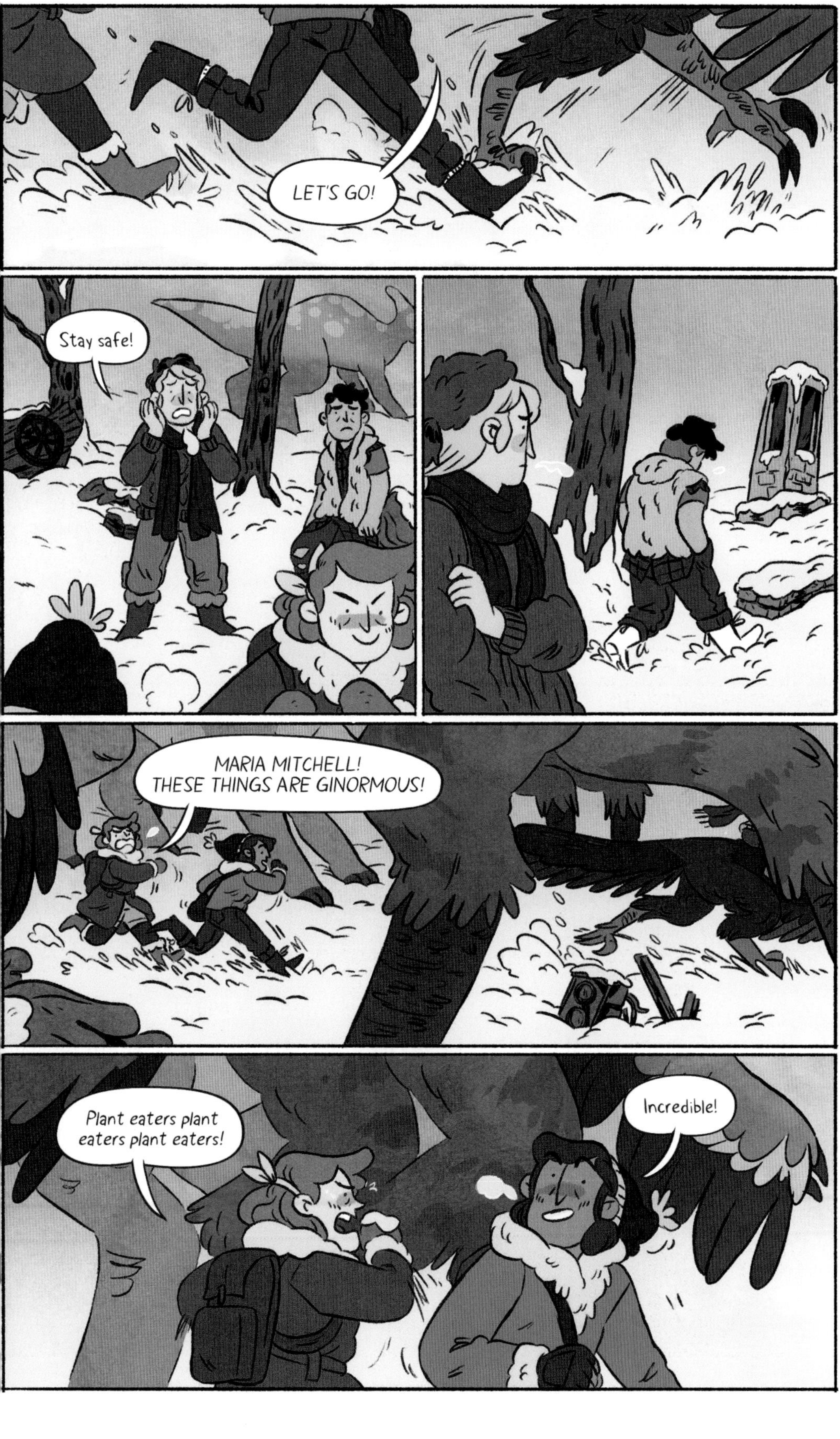
LET'S GO!
Stay safe!
MARIA MITCHELL! THESE THINGS ARE GINORMOUS!
Plant eaters plant eaters plant eaters!
Incredible!

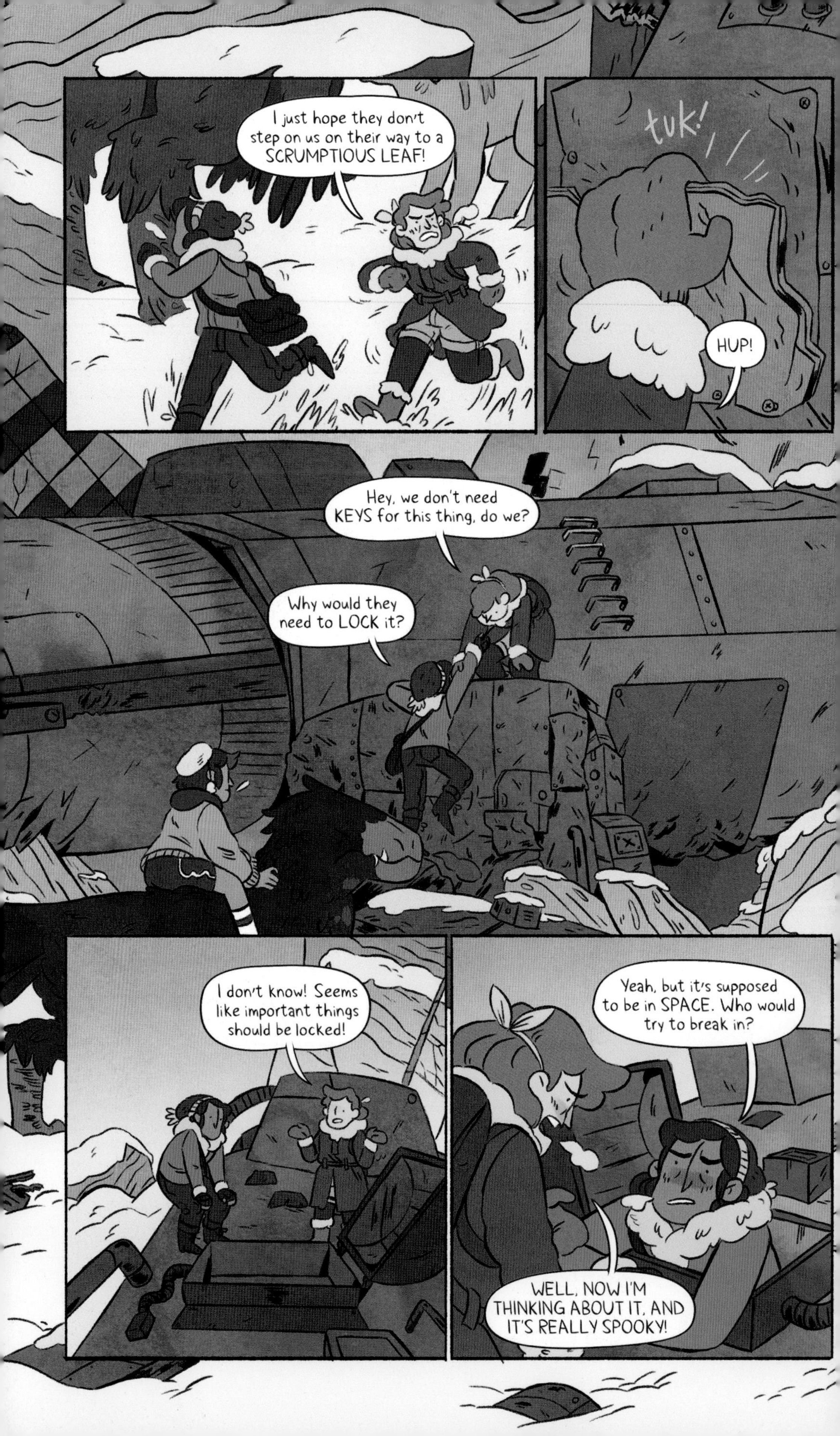
I just hope they don't step on us on their way to a SCRUMPTIOUS LEAF!
tuk!
HUP!
Hey, we don't need KEYS for this thing, do we?
Why would they need to LOCK it?
I don't know! Seems like important things should be locked!
Yeah, but it's supposed to be in SPACE. Who would try to break in?
WELL, NOW I'M THINKING ABOUT IT, AND IT'S REALLY SPOOKY!

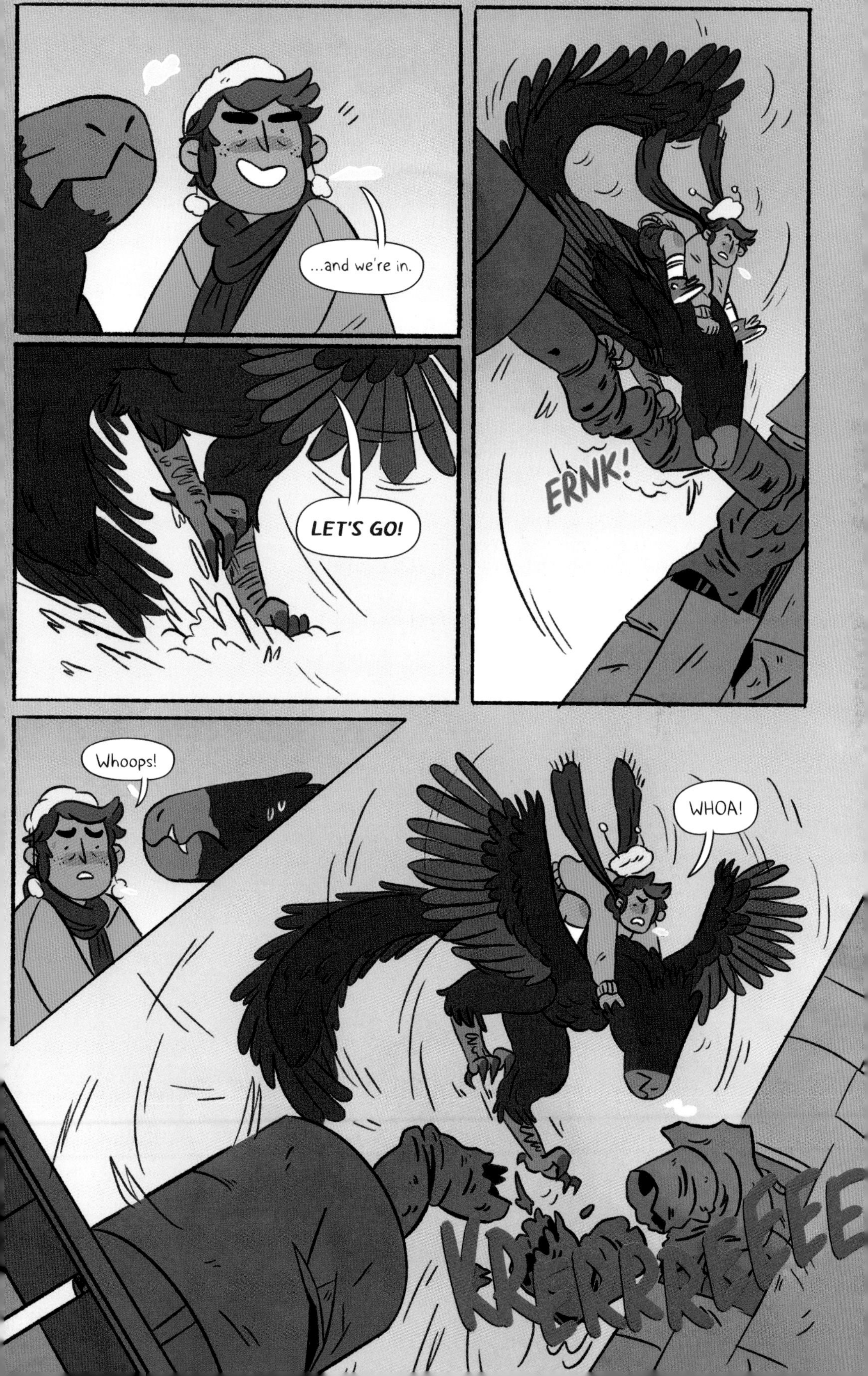
...and we're in.
LET'S GO!
ERNK!
Whoops!
WHOA!
KERRREEEE

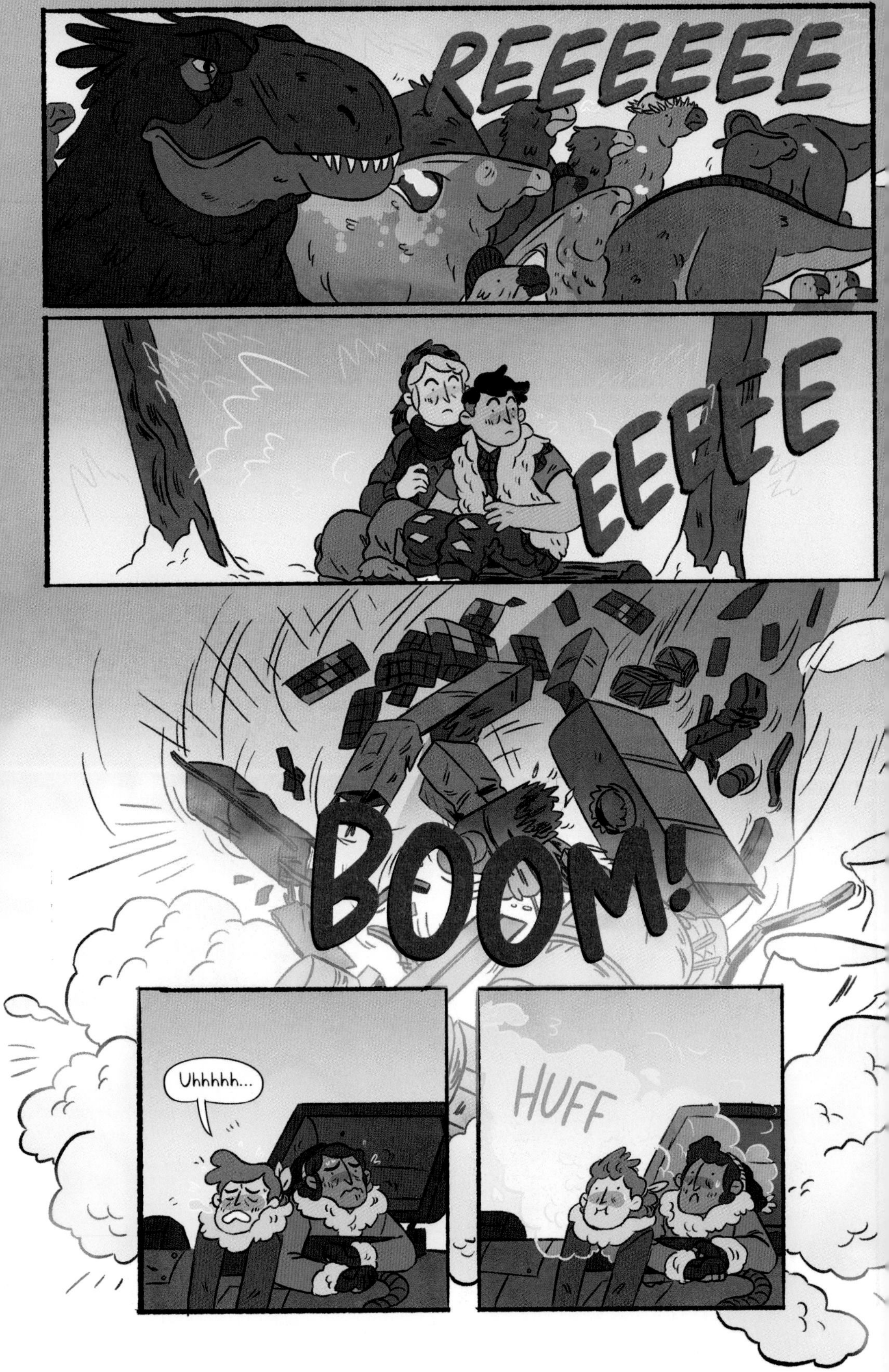
REEEEEEE
EEEEE
BOOM!
Uhhhhh...
HUFF

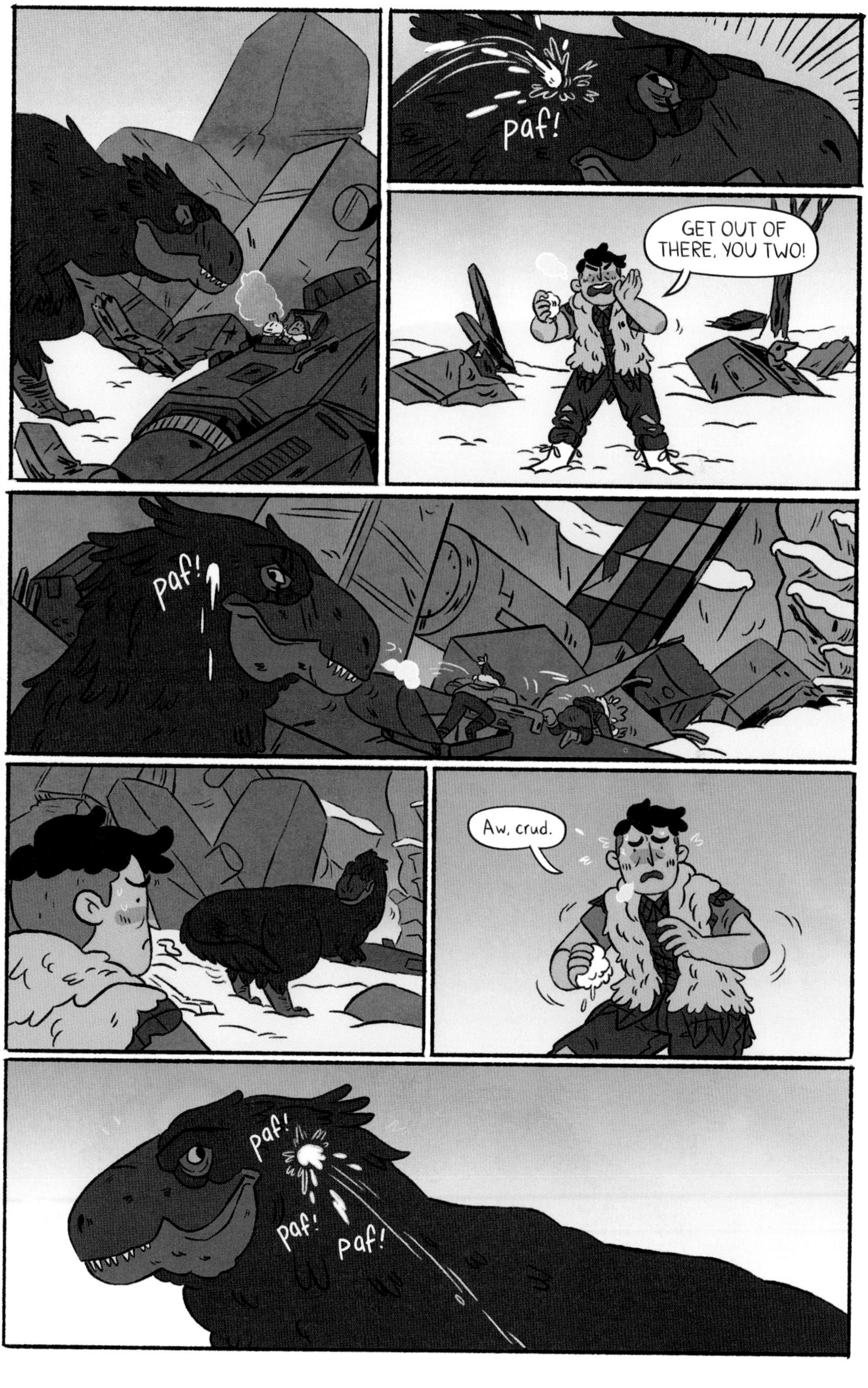
paf!
GET OUT OF THERE, YOU TWO!
paf!
Aw, crud.
paf!
paf!
paf!

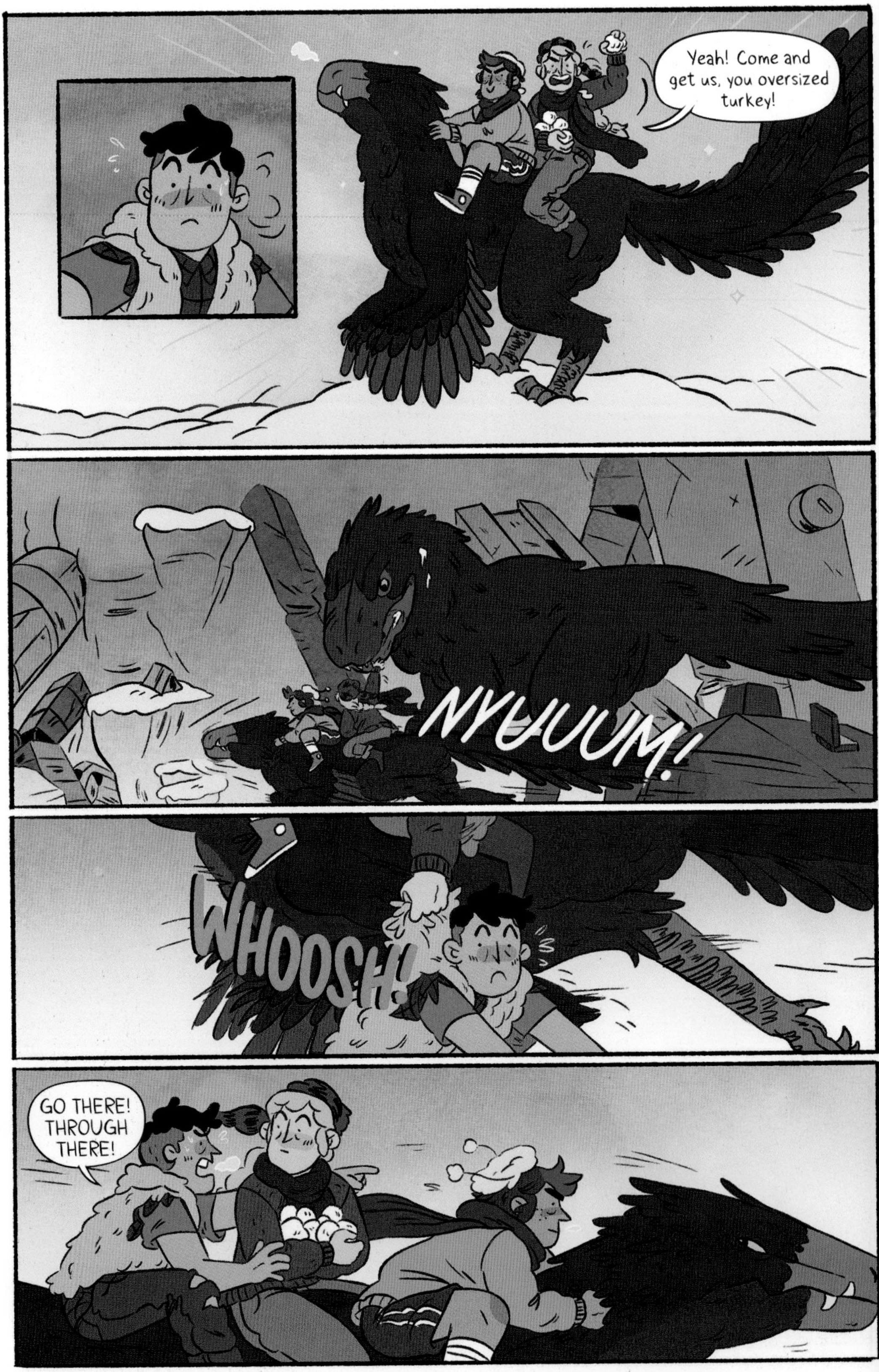
Yeah! Come and get us, you oversized turkey!
NYUUUM!
WHOOSH!
GO THERE! THROUGH THERE!

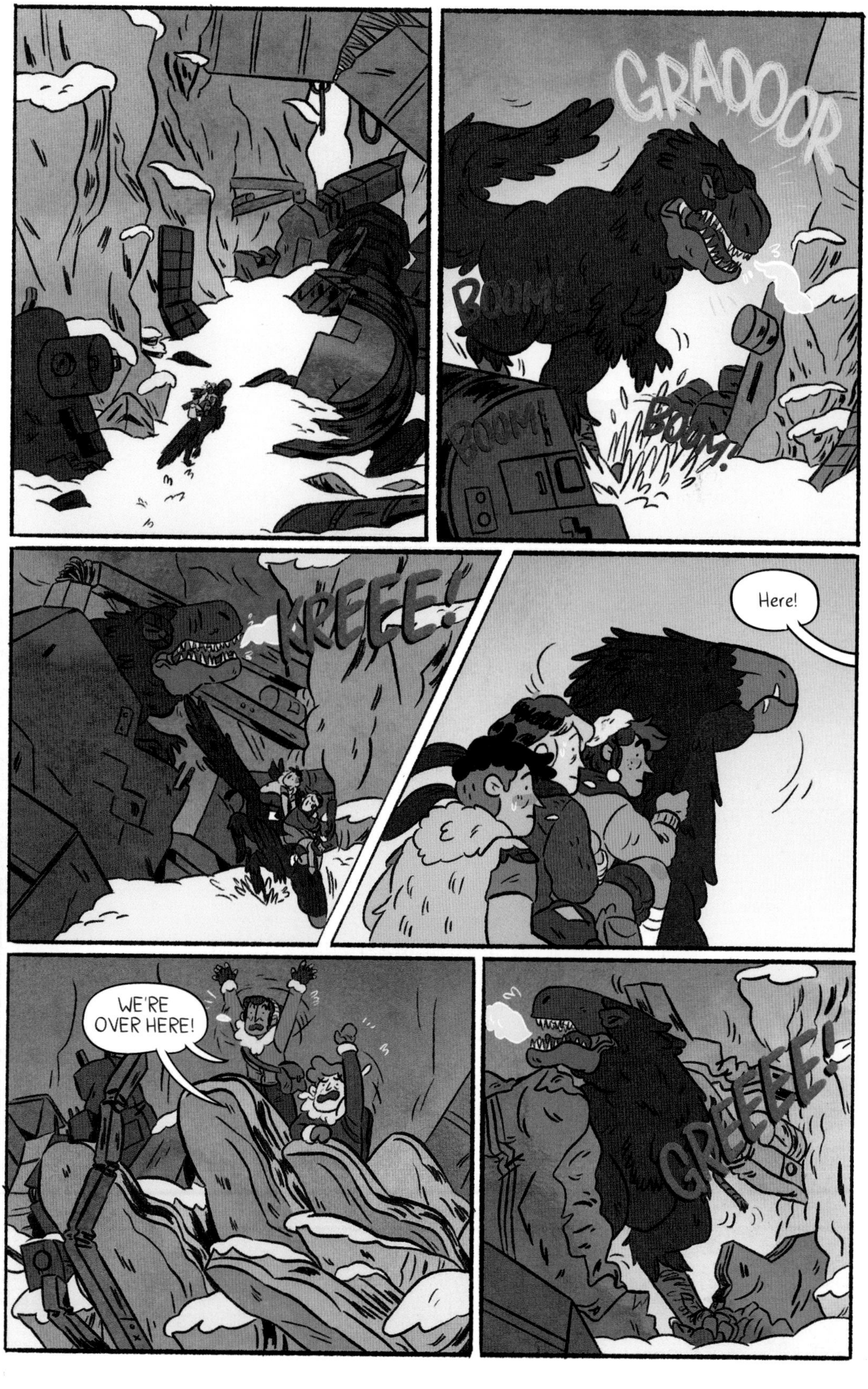
GRADOOOR
BOOM!
BOOM!
BOOM!
KREEEE!
Here!
WE'RE OVER HERE!
GREEEEE!

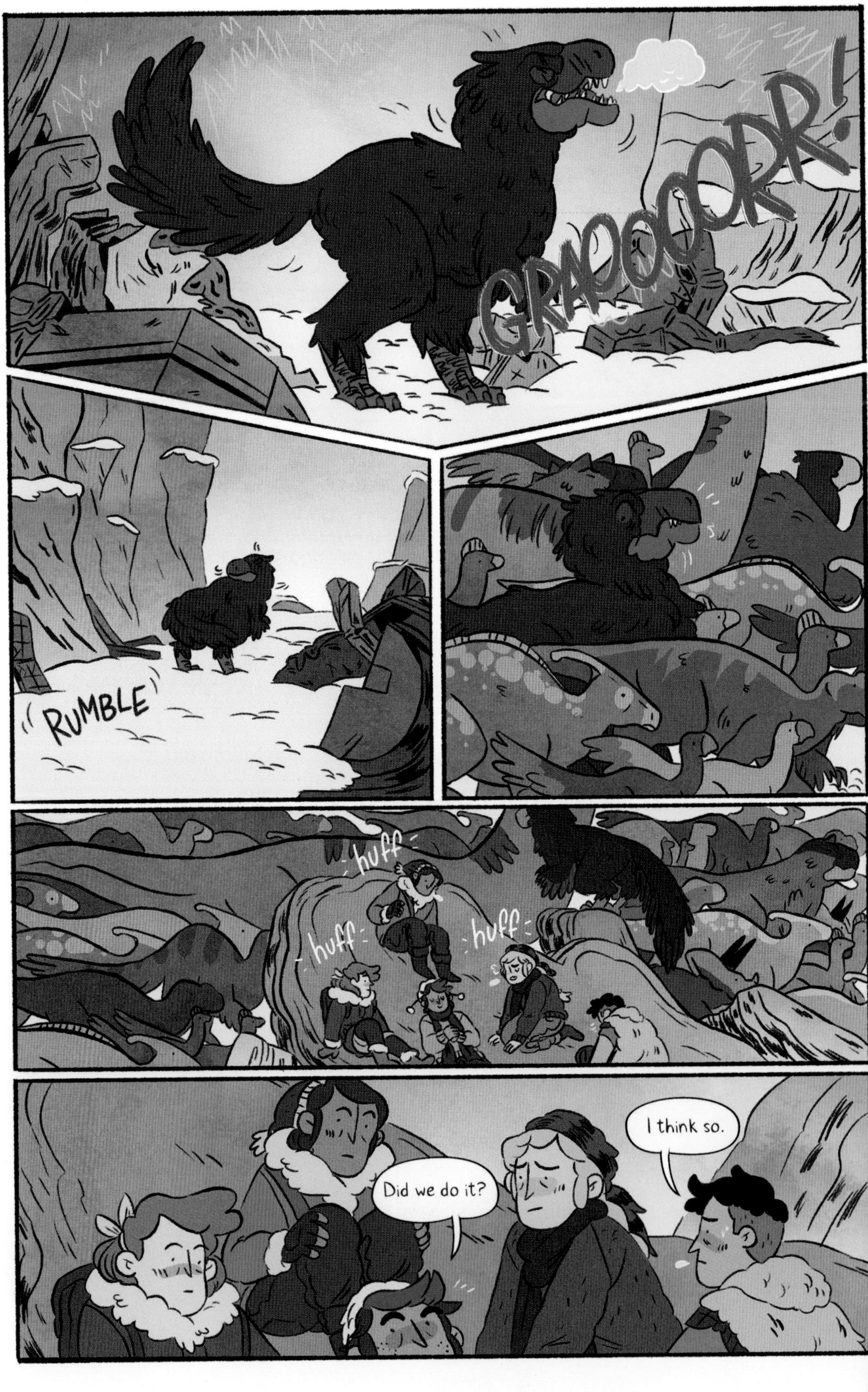
GRAOOOORR!
RUMBLE
huff
huff
huff
Did we do it?
I think so.

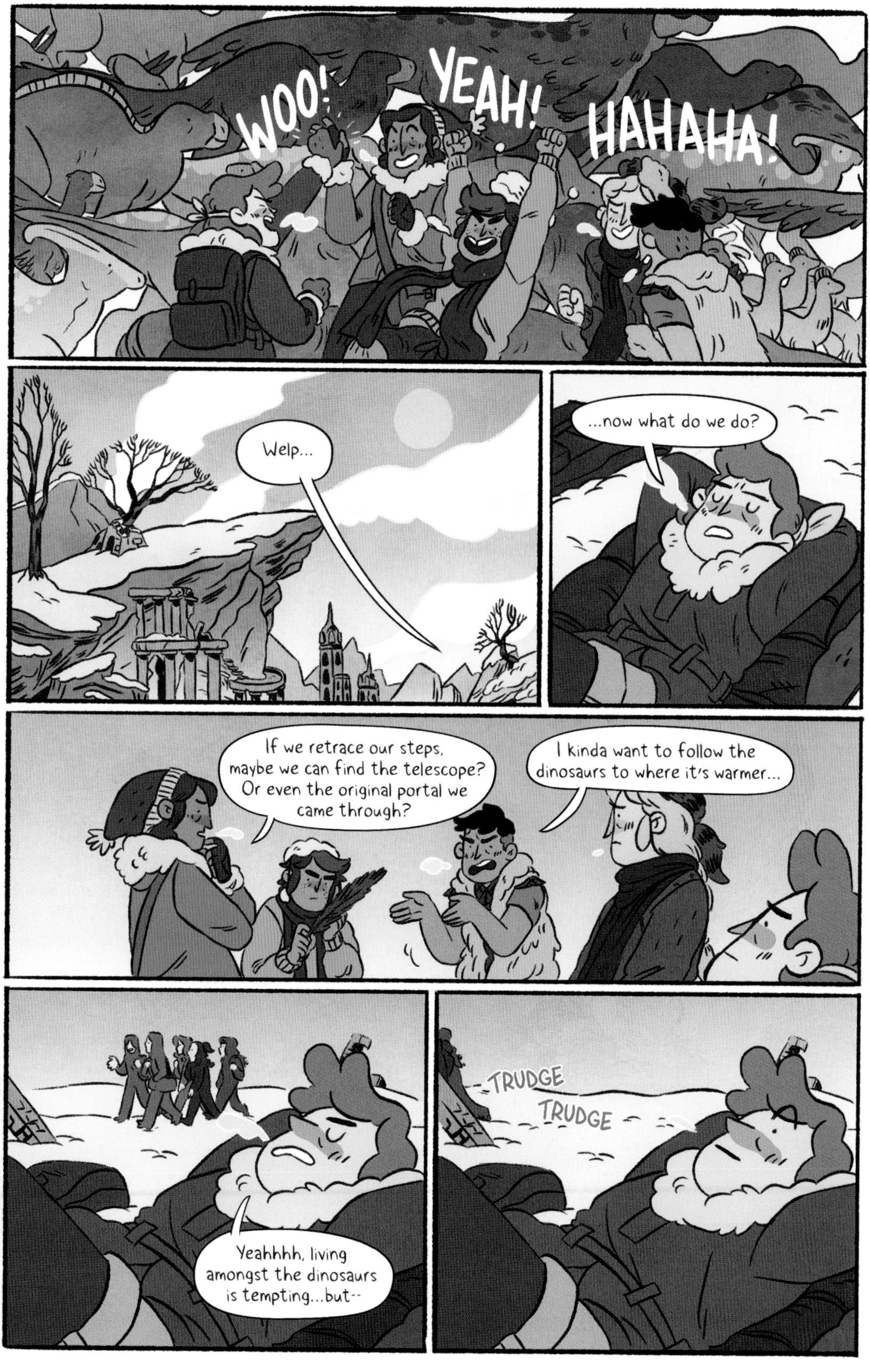
WOO!
YEAH!
HAHAHA!
Welp...
...now what do we do?
If we retrace our steps, maybe we can find the telescope? Or even the original portal we came through?
I kinda want to follow the dinosaurs to where it's warmer...
Yeahhhh, living amongst the dinosaurs is tempting...but--
TRUDGE
TRUDGE

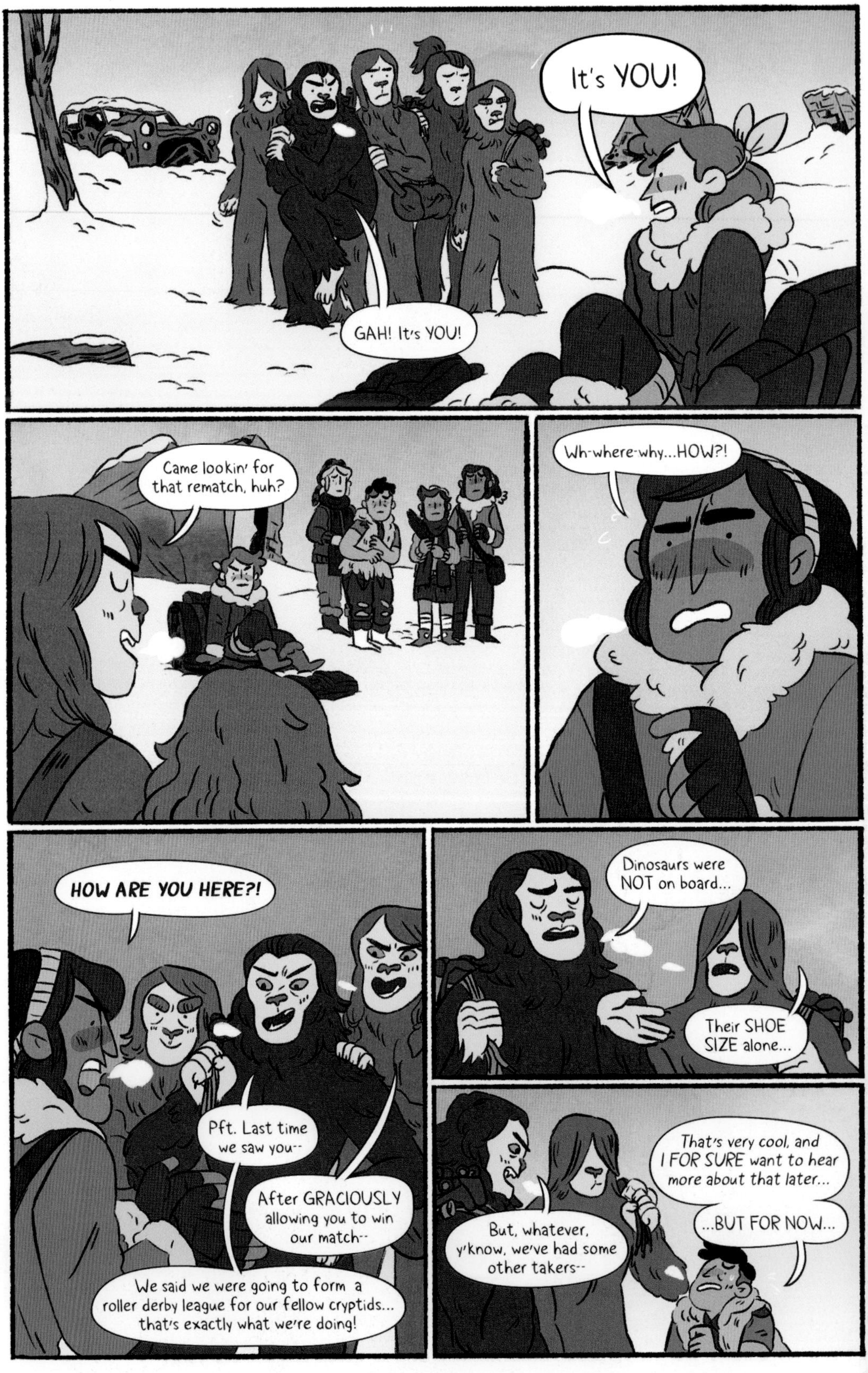
It's YOU!
GAH! It's YOU!
Came lookin' for that rematch, huh?
Wh-where-why...HOW?!
HOW ARE YOU HERE?!
Pft. Last time we saw you--
After GRACIOUSLY allowing you to win our match--
We said we were going to form a roller derby league for our fellow cryptids... that's exactly what we're doing!
Dinosaurs were NOT on board...
Their SHOE SIZE alone...
But, whatever, y'know, we've had some other takers--
That's very cool, and I FOR SURE want to hear more about that later...
...BUT FOR NOW...

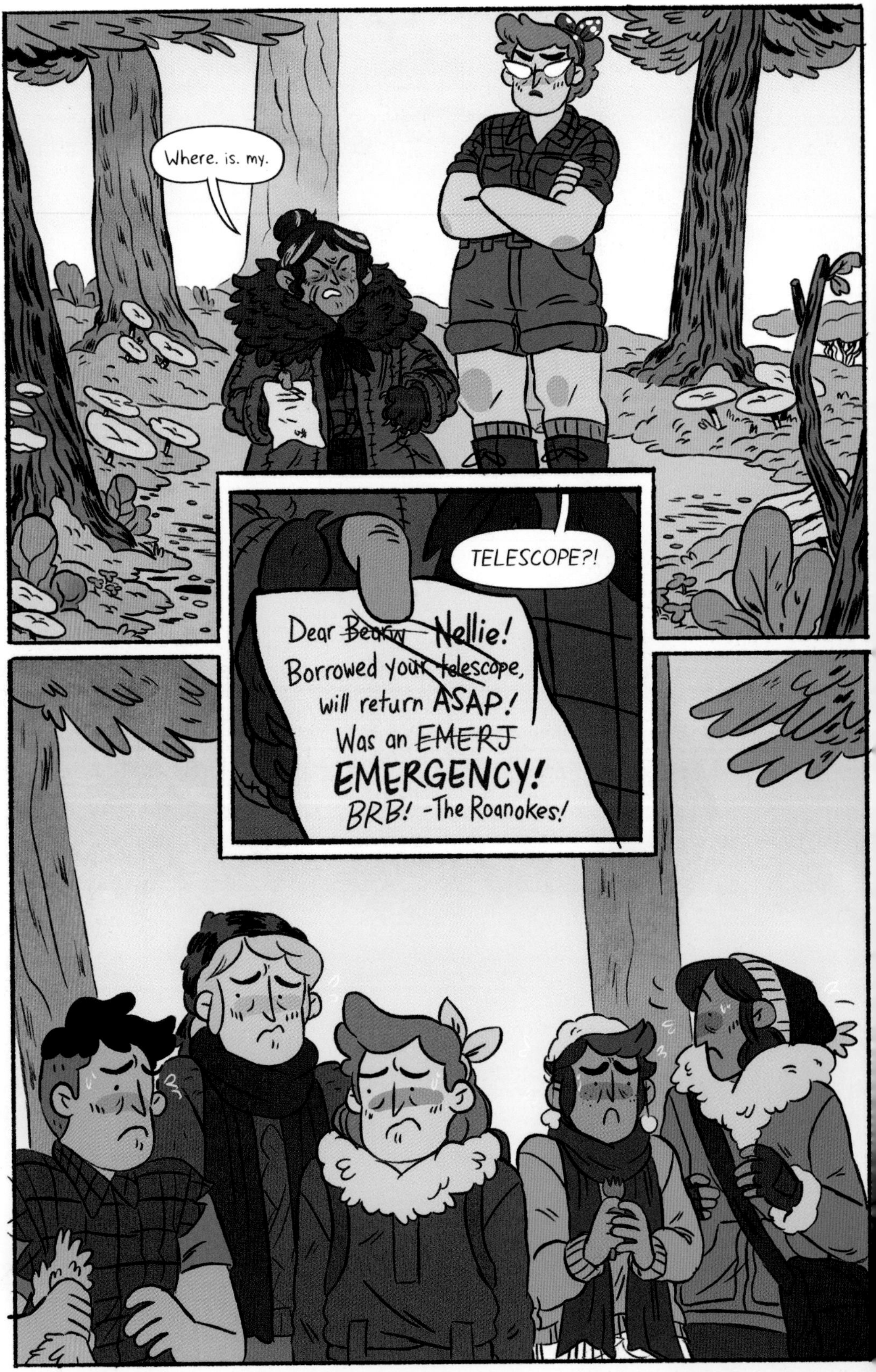
Where. is. my.
TELESCOPE?!
Dear ~~Bearw~~ Nellie!
Borrowed your ~~telescope~~ scope,
will return ASAP!
Was an ~~EMERJ~~
EMERGENCY!
BRB! -The Roanokes!

NEXT: IT'S A MYTH-TER

will co

The u

It helps

appearan

dress fo

Further

Lumber

to have

part in

Thiskv

Hardc

have

them

The

yellow, short sl

emb·

the w

choose

slacks,

made o

out-of-do

green bere

the colla

Shoes may b

heels, roun

socks should

the uniform. Ne

belong with a Lumberjane uniform.

UNIFORM

hould be worn at camp

events when Lumberjanes

may also be worn at other

ions. It should be worn as a

the uniform dress with

rrect shoes, and stocking or

out grows her uniform or

ther Lumberjane.

igma she has

her

her

HOW TO WEAR THE UNIFORM

To look well in a uniform demands first of

uniform be kept in good condition—clean

pressed. See that the skirt is the right length for your own

height and build, that the belt is adjusted to your waist,

that your shoes and stockings are in keeping with the

uniform, that you watch your posture and carry yourself

with dignity and grace. If the beret is removed indoors,

be sure that your hair is neat and kept in place with an

inconspicuous clip or ribbon. When you wear a

Lumberjane uniform you are identified as a member of

this organization and you should be doubly careful to

conduct yourself in a way that will show everyone that

courtesy and thoughtfulness are part of being a

Lumberjane. People are likely to judge a whole nation by

the selfishness of a few individuals, to criticize a whole

family because of the misconduct of one member, and to

feel unkindly toward an organization because of the

The unifor

helps to cre

in a group.

active life th

another bond

future, and pr

in order to b

Lumberjane pr

Penniquiqul Thi

Types, but m

can either bu

materials available at the trading post.

ore Lady

will wish to have one. They

uniform, or make it themselves from

The Lumberjane uniform sh... meeting...

...tivities. The ... is a bright red neckerchief is wo... neath ...uld be tied in a simple friendship knot. ...er black or brown and should have flat ...and a straight inner line. Stockings or ...pond in color with the shoes or with ...aces, bracelets, or other jewelry do not ...erjane uniform.

...WEAR THE UNIFORM

...rm demands first of all that the ...ood condition—clean and well ...t is the right length for your own ...e belt is adjusted to your waist, ...kings are in keeping with the ...ur posture and carry yourself ...ignity and grace. If the beret is removed indoors, ...e sure that your hair is neat and kept in place with an inconspicuous clip or ribbon. When you wear a Lumberjane uniform you are identified as a member of this organization and you should be doubly careful to conduct yourself in a way that will show everyone that courtesy and thoughtfulness are part of being a Lumberjane. People are likely to judge a whole nation by the selfishness of a few individuals, to criticize a whole family because of the misconduct of one member, and to feel unkindly toward an organization because of the

The helps in a g active another future in or Lumberjane ... Penniquiqul Thistle Cr... ... Types, but most Lumberjanes wi... ...ey can either buy the uniform, or make it the... ...rom materials available at the trading post.

COVER GALLERY

Lumberjanes "Out-of-Doors" Program Field

THE FRIGHT STUFF

"Fortune favors the bold."

Whether it's creepy crawlies or scary skeletons, there are more foibles and phobias in this world than there are letters in the word hippomonstrosesquippedaliophobia, a term which unfortunately means the fear of long words. Fear is a powerful and universal teacher. It protects us, reminds us of threats we've faced and ways we've kept ourselves safe. It keeps us alert for things we should beware of, situations to avoid, and people to distrust.

Many fears should be trusted. Being afraid of water may be irrational, but it also can keep us safe, whether from unknown creatures lurking in the depths, or simply from jellyfish. There are many possible ways to combat the way that your heartbeat increases and your adrenaline rises, from learning to swim better, or wearing inflatable water wings, to swimming with a little waterproof lamp for better visibility.

Some fears are more abstract—masks, or scary stories, or spider webs coating antique porcelain dollies up in the attic. These may give us the willies, but they are all the type of scary that can be fun, in the right circumstances. A thrill, rather than a chill, like a roller coaster. They become a gleeful way to give yourself a fright while knowing that you are safe all along. You feel alive, and grateful that the danger is over once the story has ended, the book has been shut tight, and the lights are all turned on again.

Plenty of fears, when pushed up against in a safe and planned way, are worth facing. Whether it's to learn to embrace new experiences and adventures, or to feel less fearful in your daily life, or even just to understand more about yourself, and why you were frightened in the first place.

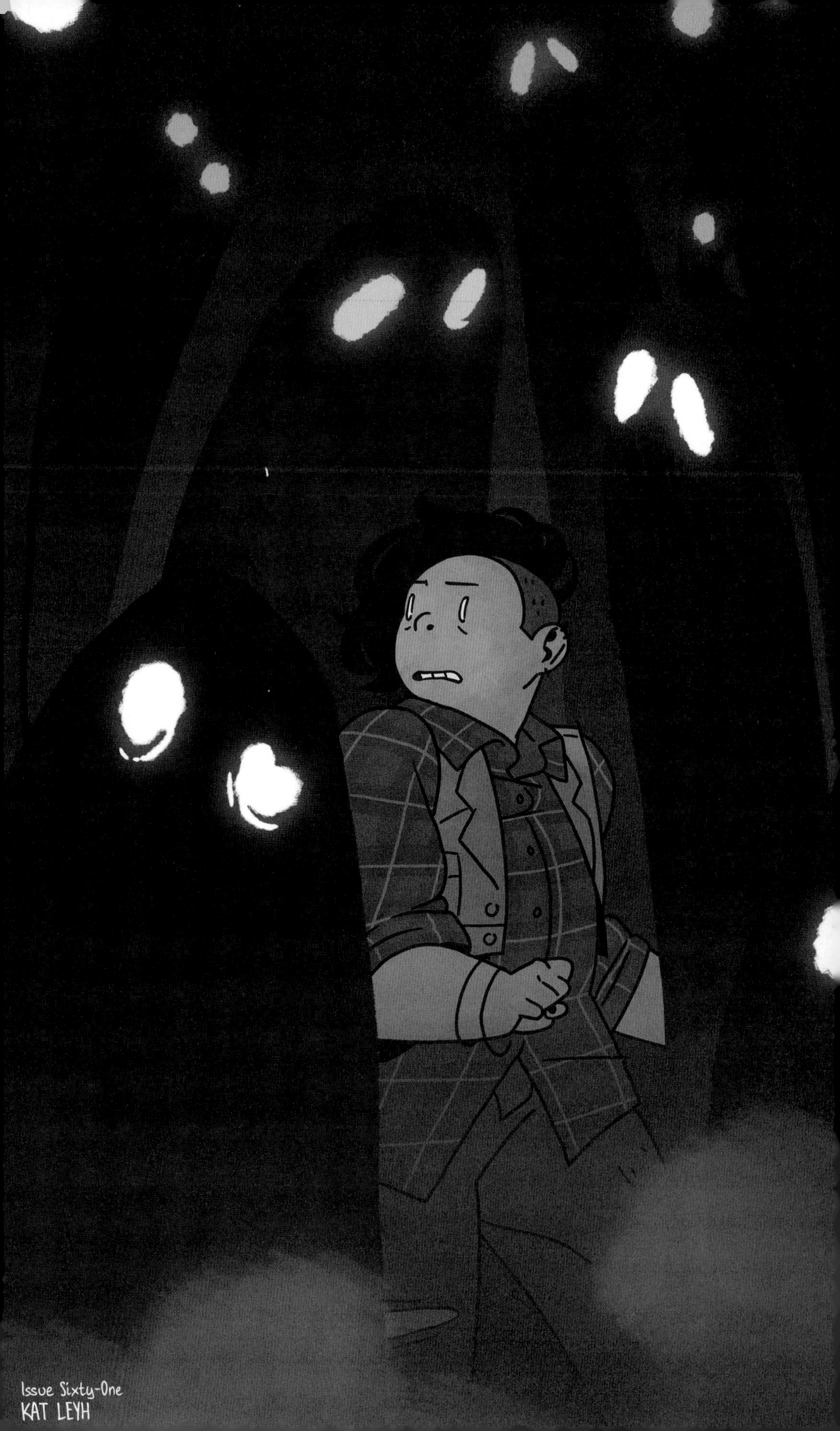

Issue Sixty-One
KAT LEYH

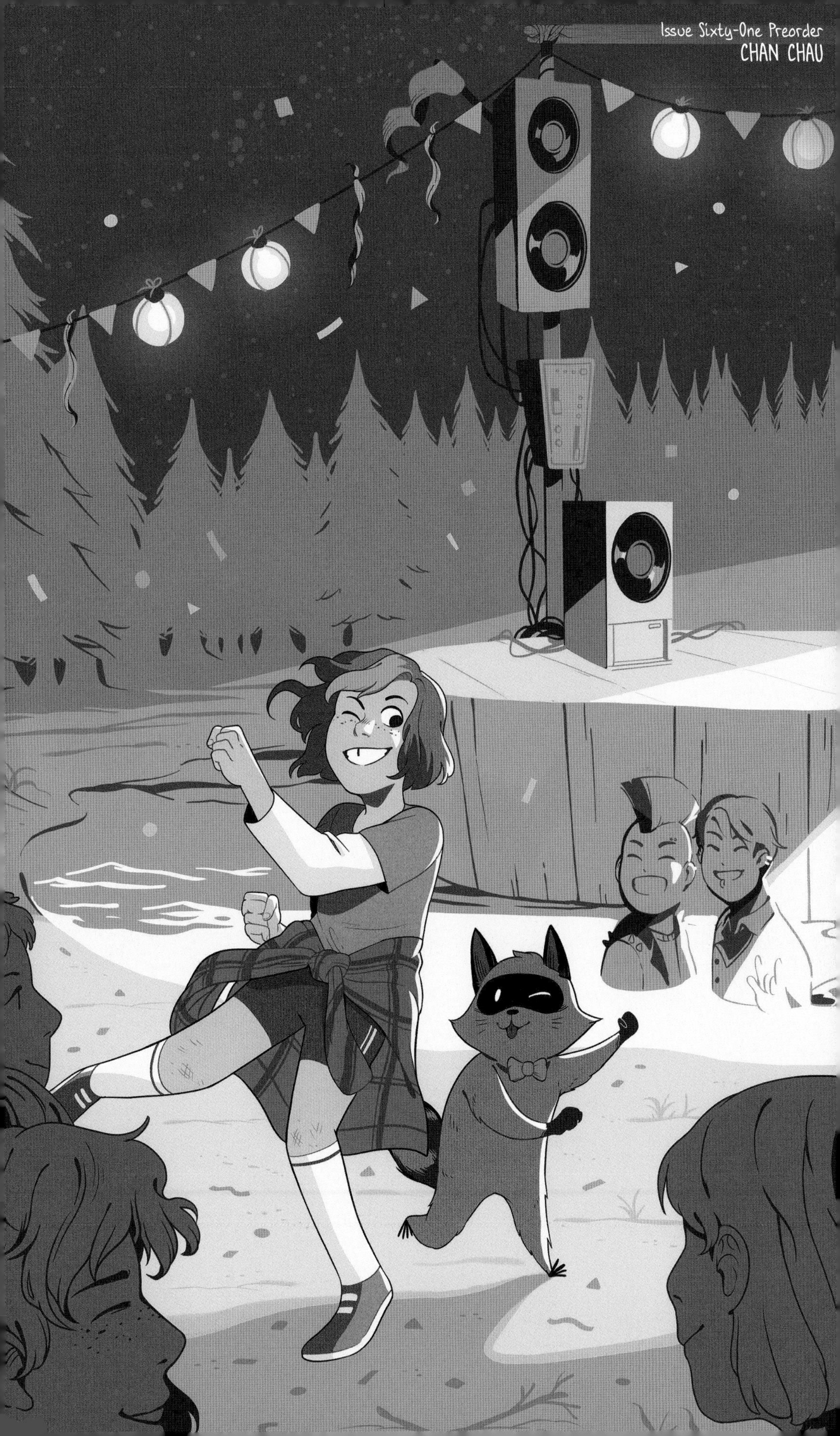

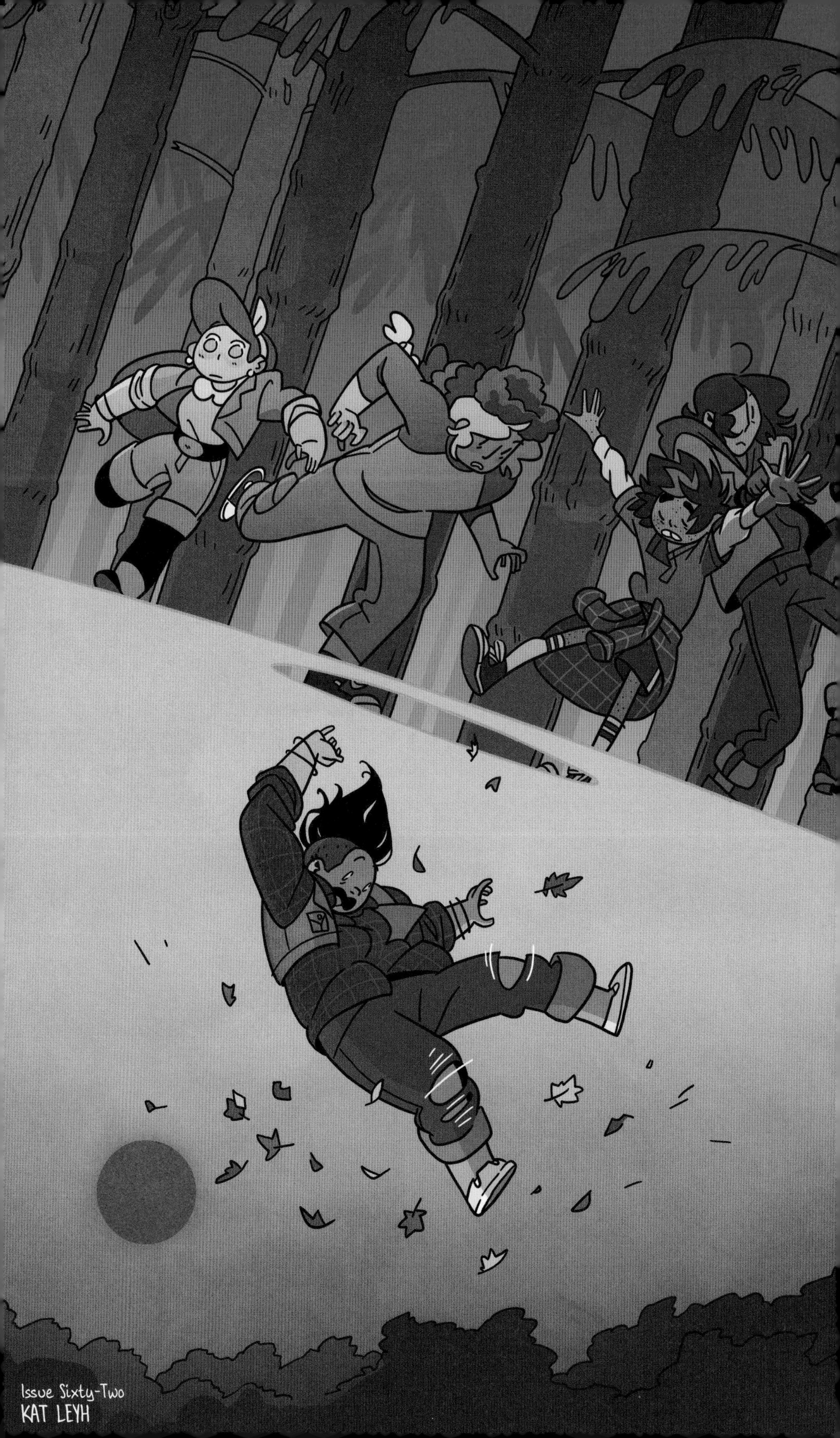
Issue Sixty-Two
KAT LEYH

Issue Sixty-Two Preorder
CHAN CHAU

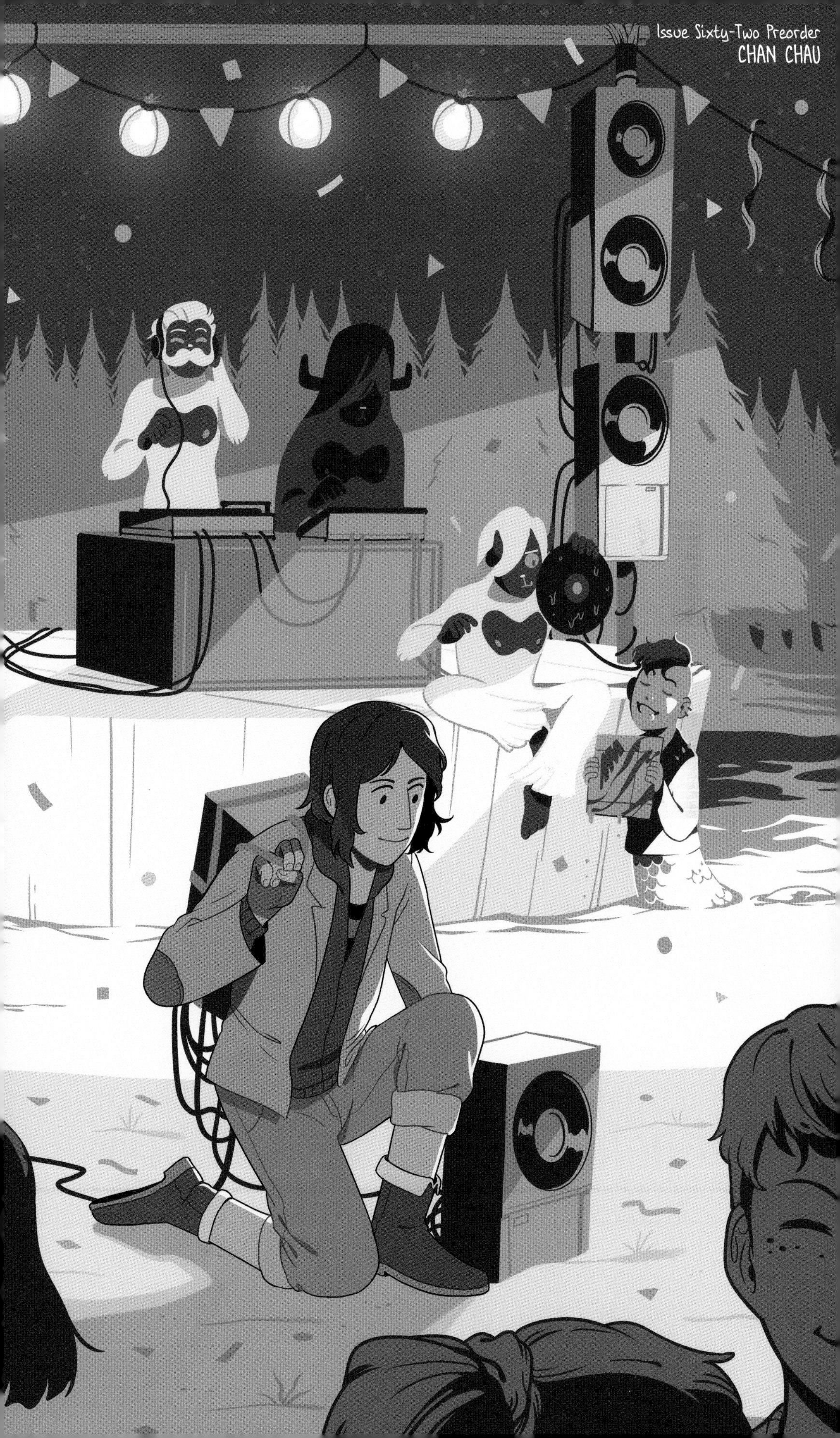

Issue Sixty-Three
KAT LEYH

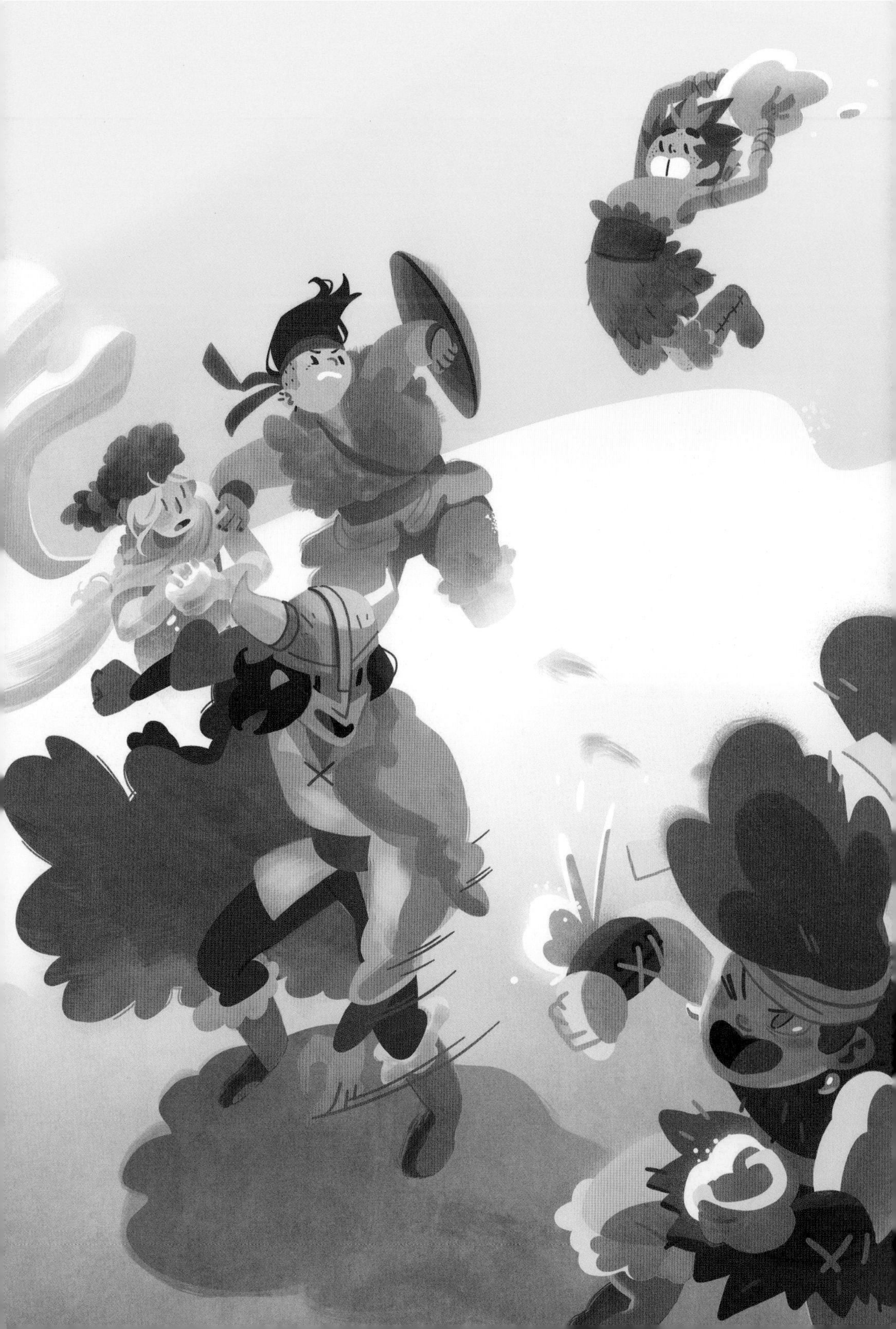

Issue Sixty-Three Preorder
CHAN CHAU

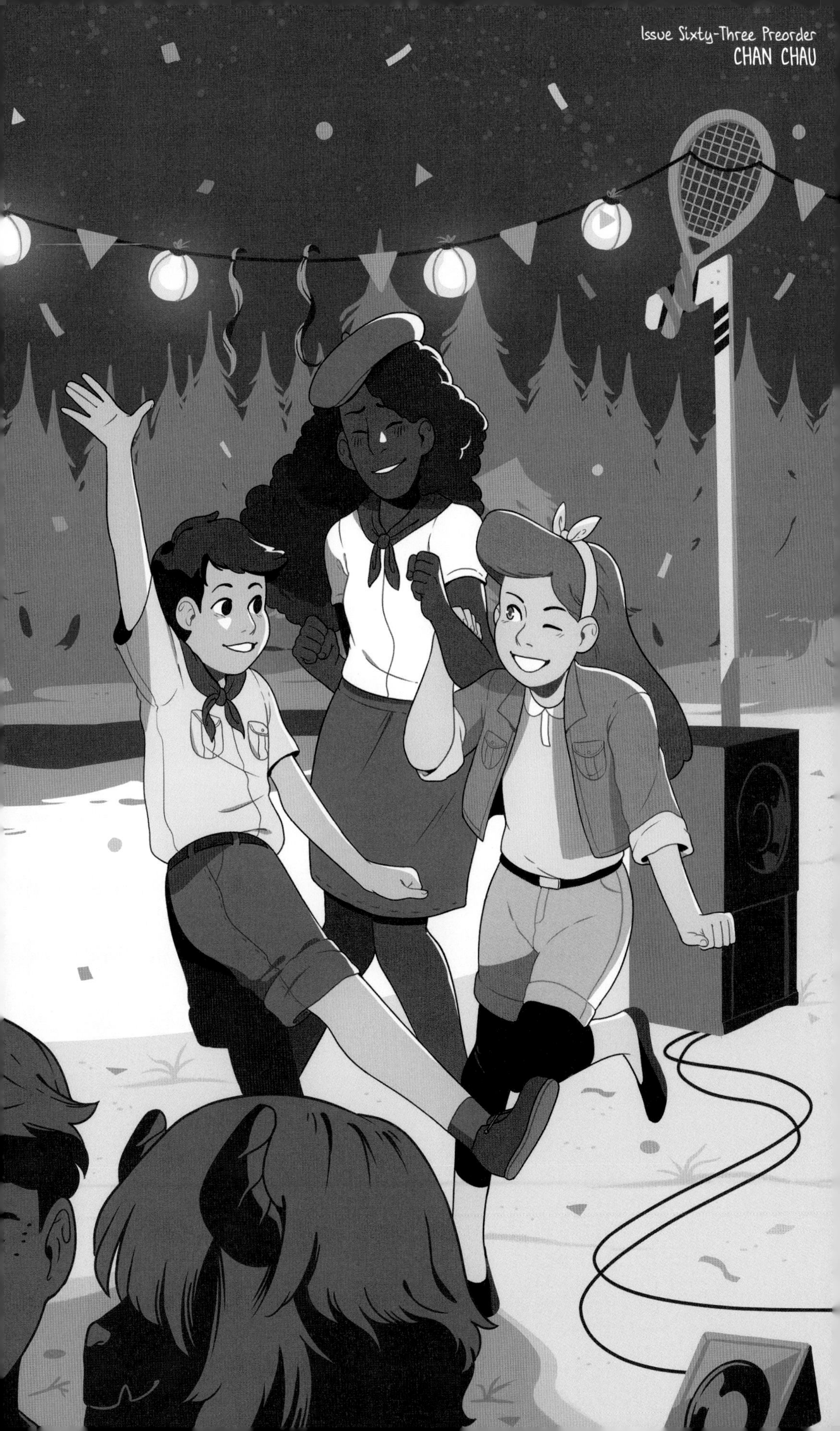

Issue Sixty-Four
KAT LEYH

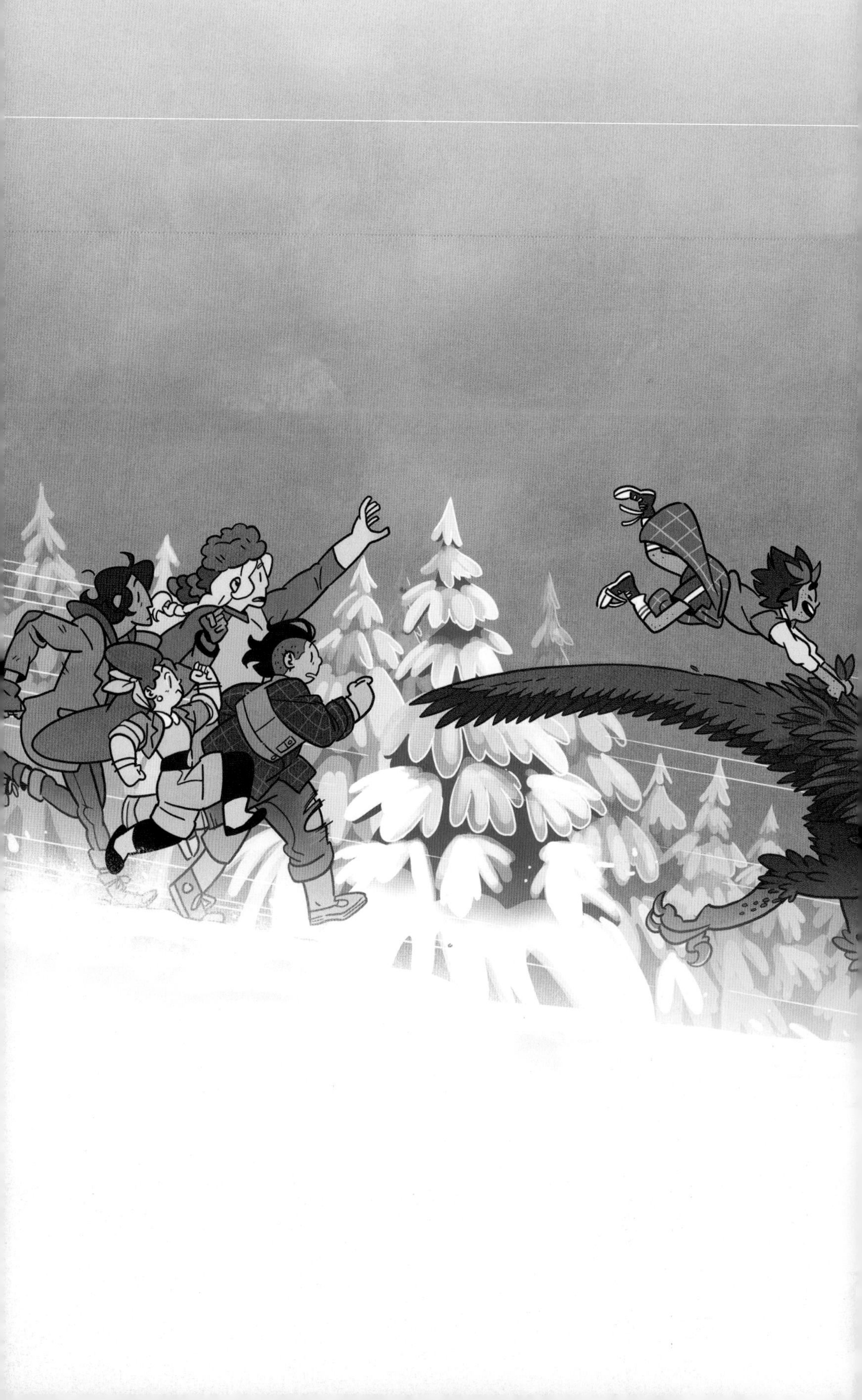

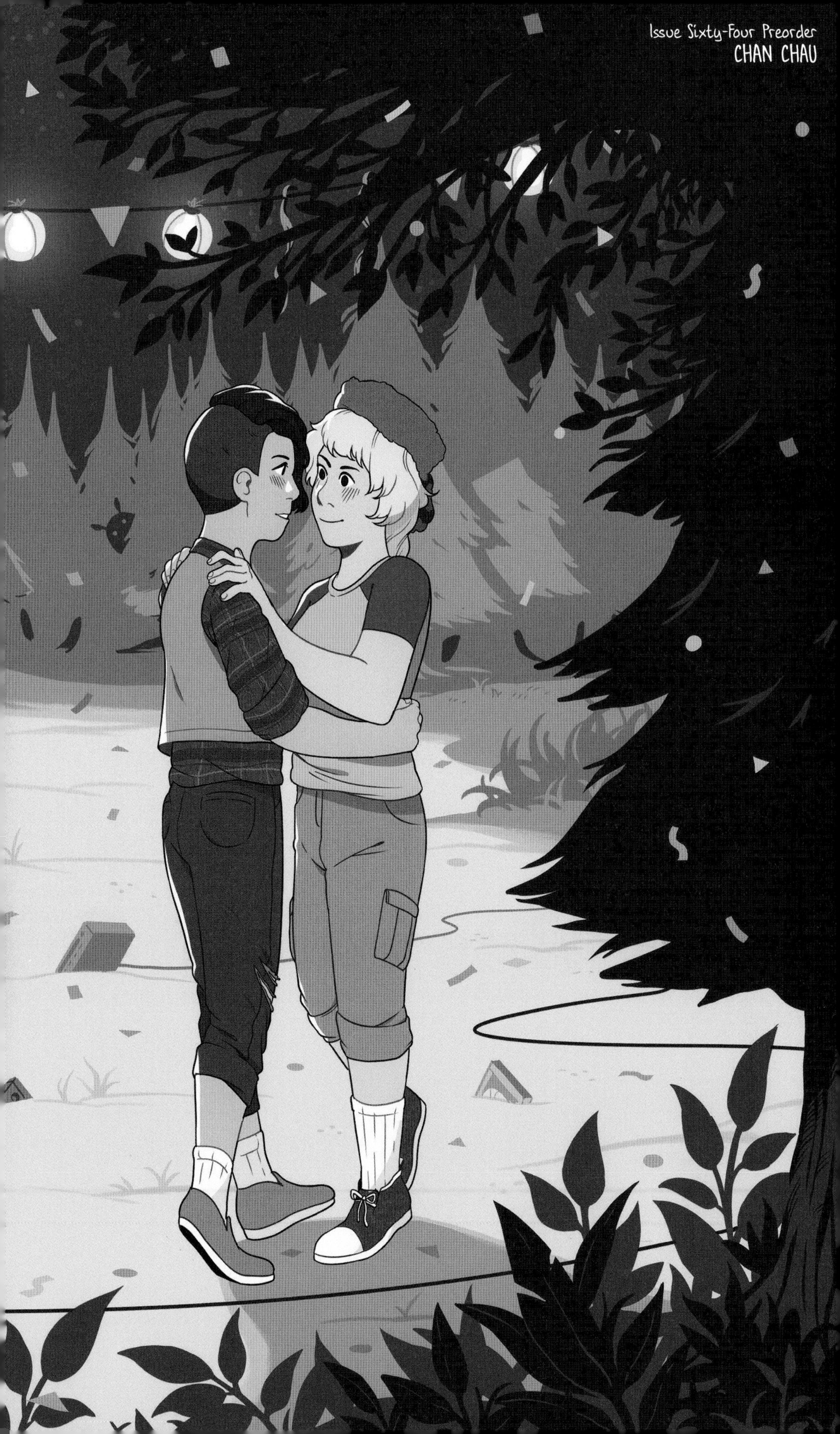
Issue Sixty-Four Preorder
CHAN CHAU

DISCOVER
ALL THE HITS

STEVENSON · ELLIS · WATTERS · ALLEN
LUMBERJANES
BEWARE THE KITTEN HOLY
NEW YORK TIMES BESTSELLING SERIES

Allison + Treiman + Cogar
GIANT DAYS
VOLUME ONE

From a writer of Disney's Moana
RIBON • FISH • PEER
SLAM!
VOLUME ONE

Hope Larson · Brittney Williams · Sarah Stern
GOLDIE VANCE
"Scoot over Nancy Drew..."
—Los Angeles Times
Volume One

JAMES TYNION IV • RIAN SYGH • WALTER BAIAMONTE
THE BACKSTAGERS

TYSON HESSE'S
DIESEL
IGNITION

Lumberjanes
Noelle Stevenson, Shannon Watters, Grace Ellis, Brooklyn Allen, and Others
Volume 1: Beware the Kitten Holy
ISBN: 978-1-60886-687-8 | $14.99 US
Volume 2: Friendship to the Max
ISBN: 978-1-60886-737-0 | $14.99 US
Volume 3: A Terrible Plan
ISBN: 978-1-60886-803-2 | $14.99 US
Volume 4: Out of Time
ISBN: 978-1-60886-860-5 | $14.99 US
Volume 5: Band Together
ISBN: 978-1-60886-919-0 | $14.99 US

Giant Days
John Allison, Lissa Treiman, Max Sarin
Volume 1
ISBN: 978-1-60886-789-9 | $9.99 US
Volume 2
ISBN: 978-1-60886-804-9 | $14.99 US
Volume 3
ISBN: 978-1-60886-851-3 | $14.99 US

Jonesy
Sam Humphries, Caitlin Rose Boyle
Volume 1
ISBN: 978-1-60886-883-4 | $9.99 US
Volume 2
ISBN: 978-1-60886-999-2 | $14.99 US

Slam!
Pamela Ribon, Veronica Fish, Brittany Peer
Volume 1
ISBN: 978-1-68415-004-5 | $14.99 US

Goldie Vance
Hope Larson, Brittney Williams
Volume 1
ISBN: 978-1-60886-898-8 | $9.99 US
Volume 2
ISBN: 978-1-60886-974-9 | $14.99 US

The Backstagers
James Tynion IV, Rian Sygh
Volume 1
ISBN: 978-1-60886-993-0 | $14.99 US

Tyson Hesse's Diesel: Ignition
Tyson Hesse
ISBN: 978-1-60886-907-7 | $14.99 US

Coady & The Creepies
Liz Prince, Amanda Kirk, Hannah Fisher
ISBN: 978-1-68415-029-8 | $14.99 US

BOOM! BOX™

AVAILABLE AT YOUR LOCAL COMICS SHOP AND BOOKSTORE

To find a comics shop in your area, visit www.comicshoplocator.com

WWW.**BOOM-STUDIOS**.COM

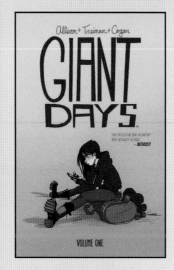

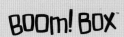